RICHARD HERRON

Copyright Notice

Copyright

The author and publisher have provided this book to you for personal use only. You may not make this book publicly available in any way. Copyright infringement is against the law. If you believe the copy of this book you are reading infringes on the authors copyright, please notify the publisher.

Table Of Contents

This book is dedicated to:

My Wife Vicki
My Daughter Aydan
My Son Liam

Know… that I love you

Shirley Moocheweinies,
an Angel that walks among us
who always gives of her heart… always

Prologue

1536 is a story that continues the early exploration and settlement of Canada by the French. The expedition leader of the voyagers was Jacques Cartier; this was to be his third and final voyage to the lands that will be known as Canada. This was a time when Aboriginals and the French were just meeting… a friendly time of exploring and trading in Canada's history.

This story turns into a rescue mission when three of Jacque's men do not return after being sent to scout further west, further than anyone had ever travelled before. Fortier has been tasked by Jacques Cartier to take his men and rescue the missing scouting party.

Travel the vast lands of Canada during its harsh winter with the French pioneers, as they explore further west in an unknown territory. The sites are beautiful, but the journey is found to be treacherous… and then a spiritual nightmare unfolds. Fortier and his men find themselves unknowingly crossing into the Aboriginal spirit world in order to continue their search, trying to rescue the scouting party that had not returned.

Exploration… to rescue mission… to horror story.

The date is February 16th of 1536 and Jacques Cartier of France is leading his third and final expedition into a land described as Kanata, unknowingly meant "Village" to the Aboriginals of these lands; the actual name of their land is Turtle Island… North America in its entirety. On the third expedition across the Atlantic Ocean the Voyagers landed on the coast, via the St. Lawrence River. Jacques was the first to set eyes on what is now referred to as Quebec City, but he wanted to venture further west; to make his mark on this land as far inland as possible. From this strong hold he sent a scouting party of three people, Tarin, Andre, and Dumont, with the orders,

"Travel four days west, make a journal of what you see in those lands; and I will expect your return on the eighth day with a full report of your findings... I will then send a full voyager expedition out after your return." stated Jacques.

On the ninth day... no one would return...

"Fortier, assemble a six man rescue crew... gather twelve days of supplies and leave at dawn... go find our men." ordered Jacques.

"Right away sir." responded Fortier.

The Brotherhood Of Men

Fortier is Jacques lead hand in all operations of his expeditions, organizing and carrying out day to day orders ensuring all tasks are met with refinement in detail… without failure. Fortier, a rough and rugged man who was no stranger to hardship and survival; a very strong man standing five foot seven inches tall; baring very callused hands that show scaring of winters cracking of his skin tissues. Long brown hair that matched the length of his very full large beard which was frosted and icy from the days winter chill on his breath. Dawning a brown worn leather jacket, with leather tassels dangling and swaying from his movements; and a fur trader's hat made of a bears hide to keep winters worst elements at bay. He and his men dress very differently than they had in France, they all dressed for the weather of this very different part of the world; clothes they had made by seamstresses copying the styles of the aboriginals for warmth.

Fortier enters the dining hall where a mixture of eighty men and women sit and eat to consume their nourishment to refuel their bodies from the day's tiresome work,

"Antin, Demarr, Marc, Basile, Tetu… gather from the cold room cellar and from the supplies storage, enough supplies for a twelve day journey; have them packed ready for dawn. We are to embark on a rescue, pack them onto five horses and ready six horses for us; be sure to pack alcohol and bandages along with other medical supplies… I don't know what kind of condition we are going to find Tarin and his scouting party in." ordered Fortier with concern in his voice.

"We will have the supplies ready before we end the day."

replied Antin.

"No indulging in drink tonight men… we have a journey ahead that is completely unknown to us and we all need to be ready for any scourge or obstacle the day might bring… sleep well." said Fortier as he left the dining hall and closed the door behind him.

Fortier walks through the log built Fort that he had helped to build on the second voyage under Jacques command. The Fort has stables for the horses, a cold cellar built underground to preserve food; a supplies store where goods are dispersed in trade for other goods or services; many small living quarters that line the Fortress walls having stoves, simple beds, shelves, a table and chairs all made by hand by those who occupy each residence. Fortier walks along a makeshift wooden walkway smiling and greeting those he crosses paths with, and finally arrives at his living quarters door. He opens the door and quickly closes it behind him to keep the winter's brisk air out as much as possible. Fortier sits at his table and lifts the glass to his lamp, striking flint onto a small mound of dried out leaves and moss; they quickly start to smolder with smoke and with a few short blows of his breath; the embers start to burn and then a tiny flame erupts. Fortier grabs a small twig and holds it to the flame and the twig ignites, Fortier quickly moves the twigs flame to the wick inside the lamp and it lights up; and he then lowers the glass filling the room with a soft glow. He leaves his chair and places moss and kindling into his stove. Fortier returns to his table and takes the lamp close to the stove, he lifts the lamps glass and lights a small twig; with the twig he lights the moss and kindling in the stove. A few moments pass and he adds small twigs and branches to the fire….and soon the crackle of the flames start to pop. Fortier walks to his shelf and takes a small pot down and sets it on the stove, he reaches over to the shelf and retrieves a jug of water and pours some water into the pot. Waiting for the water to boil, Fortier walks over and grabs four eggs he had bought from the store earlier in the day; and places them into the pot. He retrieves a plate and fork, quickly inspects them and places them at the table. Fortier walks to his small wood pile and takes six logs and places them into his stove and closes its door. The water has been boiling for a while so Fortier removes the pot from the stove and walks to the table, using his fork and thumb he removes all the eggs on to his plate; and then sets the pot on the table. With his fork he removes all of the shells from the eggs and Fortier slowly eats his night's meal in the soft light before turning in for the night.

The next morning before dawn, Fortier leaves his living quarters having already had his breakfast. He closes his door carrying this morning's coffee, sipping its greatness and waking his senses as dawn is about to rise. He is quickly met by Antin.

"The eleven horses are ready and all supplies have been loaded, we are ready sir." said Antin who was up at four AM readying the horses with the supplies by himself, to allow the others to sleep to be ready for the day's journey.

"You are a good man Antin… a great friend." replied Fortier as they walked to the stables.

The suns soft pink glow was just starting to hit the scattered clouds in the sky, the birds still asleep in their nests; no movement around the fort; smoke from the many wood stoves rises from each living quarters keeping the occupants warm in their beds; all was silent.

RICHARD HERRON

Fortier and Antin enter the corral just outside the stables where they are met by the rest of the rescue party.

"We have twelve days gentlemen… I have never failed a task and none of you have ever failed me… we are not returning until we have found or retrieved all of the scout party. We all know Tarin, Andre, and Dumont… they would do the same for any of us, so let's ration our supplies from the start and only eat and drink minimal amounts in case this drags out longer than twelve days. They have only traveled three days west maximum but we also need to keep in mind we need to search for them, and who knows how long that will take. We have winters snow to help us track them but it has now been nine days so their tracks will be minimal, if not completely wiped away from the terrain by the elements. We need to have all eyes tracking to make sure we don't miss any signs of them, the terrain will be fatiguing and grueling; there will be no paths. When we are over fatigued, us or our horses; we will stop and make camp. We need to protect us and our horses from fatigue in order to survive… are we ready?" asked Fortier in a very serious manner.

"Yes Victor, we are all ready to do anything you ask. We are prepared to face death… as brothers." replied Antin with absolution in his words.

"Then we go." said Fortier as he mounted his horse and the others also climbed their steeds; they start the trek… west.

Into The Unknown   Day One

Horses trudge through the thick powdered snow, a light breeze scatters the flakes of ice; and twinkle like stars as the sun lights the snow crystals as far as the eye can see. Small patches of brown plant life sways in the wind, waiting for winters end. Tiny black and white birds flutter from tree to tree, branch to branch; scurrying and foraging for dead of winters scraps of nourishment; they search endlessly for what has not yet been plucked; knowing if they don't hurry and eat today; they may not rise tomorrow. These lands are unforgiving to all creatures that inhabit it, and to all who wish to cross it. They meet a large wooded forest, trees tightly nestled together with very little room between the tall slender trunks; but not impassable;

"There… wrapped around that tree." said Fortier as he gives his horse a light kick with his heal causing his horse to canter quickly ahead.

Fortier pulls back on the reins forcing the horse to stop at the forest edge, he lifts his hand and holds a white torn piece of fabric that is wrapped around the tree;

"Tarin left markers!" said Fortier with a hint of relief in his voice;

"We have a chance… Antin, cut loose one of your jackets tassels and tie it around this marker… so if they come back this way they will know we have passed here." explained Fortier and Antin did as he was asked.

Fortier looked for any other signs that they may have left.

"Wait… there is another, about twenty feet into the forest… they are pointing the path they had taken; the route they have taken is tight but manageable… good thinking Tarin!" said Fortier.

"The forest is too large to go around, that's probably why

they went straight in... they had no choice... alright let's move." ordered Fortier as they slowly navigated their way through the timber filled obstacles. On ward they pressed, slowly navigating through the branches and downed tree trunks; Fortier could see a slight path that Tarin had taken. The path was not on the ground, it was the few broken branches of the trees; here and there; they were scattered but easy enough to follow as they made their way through this obstacle ridden path. Hours had passed by as they pressed on through the trees, finding Tarin's tree markers about every half hour. Down and then up the tree filled hills they had to walk their horses, leading them in tow by their reins;

"Come on boy let's go... get up there!" Fortier could be heard encouraging his horse as they climbed the hills, not an easy task for man or beast.

They reached the crest of yet another hill, Fortier stops and looks to see what the landscape could tell him, and then;

"HEY...WE ARE ALMOST THROUGH!!!" yelled Fortier in excitement.

"YAAAAAA... ALRIGHT!!!" yelled Antin, cheers quickly followed by the other men; thankful to soon be out of the thick forest.

"Looks like there is a clearing not far passed the bottom of this hill, we will make camp at the edge of the tree line... it will be dark soon." stated Fortier,

"Sounds great!" said Tarin as smiles now lit up the faces of all the men, thinking of a warm fire and warm food in their bellies.

"From up here it looks like there is a valley that curves south and then continues west... I would imagine that is the route Tarin would have taken, we will check for markers in the morning." explained Fortier.

"Open ground... sounds great to me." replied Antin with a

cheerful smile on his face.

The rescue party made their way slowly down the hillside and finally reach the bottom, they mount their horses and slowly weave through the trees for twenty minutes getting closer to the end of the tree line; Fortier stops.

"Hey, Tarin cleared this area and camped here, you can see where the ashes of his camp fire was; we will stop here." said Fortier to the delight of the party.

The men set up a lean-to made out of branches to block the cold winters wind, and started a fire to quickly get their supper started. They tied the horses to the trees and removed their saddles placing them around the fire for something dry to sit on as they warmed by the fires light. The beautiful evenings sunset had slowly diminished for the night, the nights black skies slowly cascaded their way across the heavens; chasing the suns light until it was no more. The stars appear and grow brighter as the sky turns black. No more bird calls, they have gone to sleep in their nests for the night; only the crackle of the nights fire could be heard under the jarring comradery of the men around the nights fire as they are finishing up their supper… only their laughter could be heard. *"Heyyyyyy Basile, I'm not saying she was a frog… unlike her, frogs don't have only one pretty tooth… hahahahahahahaha… and why would you always under pay her; why are you so cheap?"* joked Demarr as he and all the others laughed.

"Hahaha heyyyy… come on now ha ha… I'm not cheap… I just like it when she chases me for the rest of the money… the thumping noise of her wooden peg leg almost drives me to tears I laugh so hard hahahahahaha" roared Basile joining the others in laughter.

The laughter and jokes calm down and everyone's

drowsiness starts to catch up.

"Well the sun gets up early gentlemen and tomorrow is going to be a full day... I think it's time to rest while we can." said Fortier.

"Ya, I will throw a bunch more logs on this fire, should last the night." said Marc as he got up.

The men all gathered their saddles and placed them at the back of the lean-to for their heads to rest on and covered themselves with their blankets. Everyone was quiet…

"Madeline's wooden peg leg... " said Fortier and they all burst out laughing again, after a bit of laughing;

Fortier says as he laughs;

"Ok guys, seriously... I don't want to dream about her TOOTH!" and then they all BURST into immense laughter hurting their stomachs a little from the tightness of the muscles.

They all new that was enough joking for one night. Their feet were all positioned close to the nights fire keeping them warm… mostly. They all faded off quietly to sleep.

The Lake Of Passage   Day Two

The sun starts to peek over the hill to the east and the sky is lit with mornings pastel pink and blue colors, the light blue shadows of the trees start to grow lighter on the snow as the sun slowly rises. Tetu is extinguishing breakfast's fire and gathering the mornings dirty dishes and brings them to Basile, who was washing the mornings cook ware. The men saddle up their horses and ready themselves for the day's journey ahead. They exit the tree line and look out into the clearing,

"Well… let's make our way across this clearing to that tree line and look for more markers left by Tarin." said Fortier as he lightly kicked his horse with his heal.

They all travelled single file across the clearing, the snow was fairly deep; just past the horse's knees. Fortier didn't push the horses, he let them go at their own pace to let them conserve their energy for the day. The wind was much heavier today, blowing snow flakes across the ground sending what looks like snow snakes racing across their path; winters cold freezes each breath of man and beast; slowly taking their energy away with each shiver.

"There!" said Fortier as he seen two white markers wrapped around the tree,

"They point in the direction of the valley… that's what I thought they would do, wrap their markers… let's follow this valley east along these trees; the trees will provide a little shelter from this wind." said Fortier as he and the men started their horses moving once more.

The snow was not as thick along the trees allowing the horses to move a little more freely. Three large black birds caw at each other as they take turns pecking and tearing at the meat of the dead carcass, of the unknown animal in the distance; in the middle of

RICHARD HERRON

the snow filled clearing.

The wind starts to calm down to a light breeze and the party seems to enjoy the new scenery. Looking at the hill sides of the valley they are in, filled with large green trees covered in snow going up and over the hills.

The sun stretches the trees shadows as far as it can early this morning, small wildlife tracks can be seen in the snow; taunting the imagination of the men; like some sort of story can be told by their playful tracks left for them to see. Brown and yellow birds occasionally fly up to the tree line, chirping and dancing from branch to branch as the riders ride by; and as quickly as they arrived to say hello… they were gone back into the forest; having said what they wanted to say the strangers; and then they fluttered away to go about their days business. Twisting and turning with the valley, the men rode and followed the path that the valley had cut for them. Out in the distance, a large group of eighteen deer stare at the men; then quickly they all hopped and jumped to hide in the forest trees. They were still finding the markers left behind by Tarin which kept the men's spirits high, knowing that they were on the path of those they were to rescue.

A few miles through this valley and most of the day has been spent, a wondrous scenery that fills the men's hearts; the beauty of this land is captivating; and also the men knew that this land could be unforgiving and treacherous.

"Look… it looks like there is a lake up ahead… we will stop there and see which direction Tarin had taken." said Fortier as the party pressed on through the snowy terrain.

"Sounds good, the horses could use a rest." replied Antin.

A little further they traveled, steadily toward the ice and

RICHARD HERRON

snow

RICHARD HERRON

covered Lake; reeds and cat tails surround the edge of the lake; poking out of the snow in bushels. The men notice two white rabbits chasing each other, they too seem to be enjoying the day; hopping, bounding, and chasing each other in a playful manner; paying no attention to the men as they approach from afar. They round a bend very close to the lake, exposing more of the hidden lake as they approached; closer and closer to the icy edge.

"Fortier look... what is that?" asked Demarr with a horrified tone in his voice.

The party came to a sudden halt. The men stop in their tracks and can only stare, a few meters away from the lakes edge they see large trees that seem out of place; like they were planted and grown specifically in their place with reason. The trees were spread apart in a very even manner, in a very large scale rectangle; but there was something very bizarre about this place. There was a very obvious entrance to the site, the two tree trunks at the entrance went up eight feet and then as if they were bent or encouraged to grow horizontal; and made to weave through the other trees; all the way around this site. Skeletons of large animals…bears, cougars, buffalo, wolves, moose, and elk all could be seen crammed together on the two entrance trees; like they were spirits to ward off evil spirits.

"Let's go check and see what's inside." said young Tetu in an excited voice.

"No, we are not going in there!" said Fortier in a very stern voice.

"It looks like a very old burial site… can't you see the hundreds of large humps in the snow inside the site, I am guessing those are burial stones; the way those trees have been made to grow around the site like that must have been started… probably a few hundred years ago. It could STILL be an active grave site for

the indigenous peoples in this area… none of us are going to enter that site… we are going to travel well away from that site and go around it." said Fortier with great concern in his voice.

The men understood by the tone of Fortier's voice, the level of respect and a bit of fear that was going through Fortier's mind; and none of the men dared to question any further about the matter.

"I wanted to stop here and ready camp… but because of this site we are going to travel on the lake and go well around the site. When we get far enough away, we will set up camp." stated Fortier.   *"Why are you being so cautious… are you afraid of ghosts hahaha."* joked Basile.

"If this is an active grave site… that means the indigenous peoples are not far from here, and that means there is a chance that they will see our tracks in the snow and if they see that we went anywhere near that site… they would probably hunt us down and kill us all… probably in our sleep; they could be watching us all right now and we would never know it… so like I said… we are going to travel WELL AWAY from that site; or we could become ghosts ourselves." said Fortier with absolution in his voice.

All of the men started shifting their eyes, staring into the wooded forest that surrounds them from both sides; not moving their heads; trying not to look like they were searching the forest for anyone watching them and their every move.

"Ok… stop looking into the forest men, if they are watching us you will never find them; let's just head straight out onto the ice and hope they see our good intentions… and hopefully they don't hunt us down and kill us anyway." said Fortier giving the men the bad news as strait forward as he could.

They head out onto the solid snow covered ice.

"Spread out a ways apart… I don't want this ice cracking from all of our weight." ordered Fortier as he started into the ice

RICHARD HERRON

with his horse.

The men all waited as each took their turn going onto the ice, waiting a while for each man to get a ways away before taking their turn tempting the lakes icy surface. As they made their way on the snow and ice, they would hear cracks that would ressinate a sound off in a direction of its choosing; which kind of sounded like a bullet ricochet under the ice; it was very unpredictable and very un-nerving for the men. Single file they tredged on, hoping the lakes ice would serve its purpose as they followed Fortier's lead; they were nearing the half way mark of the lake.

"Alright, we are going to start heading toward the shore line." yelled Fortier to his men as he made a slight change in direction, a slow and steady path made by Fortier through the heavy snow.

As they reached the lakes edge Fortier looked at the tree line, *"Set up camp just inside those trees... the sun will be down soon so we need to hurry."* explained Fortier.

"Demarr, Tetu and I will collect firewood; and wood for the lean-to; Marc and Basile tend to the horses and get the fire going to start preparing supper." ordered Antin so that there was no confusion and things were done quickly.

"With the little amount of daylight we have left, I am going to travel a little further up the tree line to see if there are any markers that can be seen... I should only be a short while." said Fortier assuring the men he would not be very long.

Fortier continued to the tree line searching for markers, along the way Fortier was glaring into the forest... searching for tracks of Tarin and his men; but his eyes also searched for any indigenous people hidden in the forest. Fortier seen tracks of the wood land creatures that ventured these woods... seems like the forest is bountiful, on all levels of the food chain.

"There it is." said Fortier as he now has a destination to fixate on, focused on the marker that lies just ahead.

Wrapped around the tree, Fortier finds the tattered piece of cloth waving in the wind; waving at its command. Fortier stops at the marker and looks further down the tree line, and he sees the second marker.

"Ok, we have our heading." says Fortier to himself with relief.

Fortier has another quick look around to see what he can see as light is growing more scarce, he motions and moves to turn his horse.

"WAIT!" Fortier commands his horse.

"What is that?" said Fortier as he gets down from his horse to get a closer look at something that caught his eye in the snow.

Fortier bends down and sees a large deep print in the snowy surface. These tracks were unfamiliar to Fortier, they were not of a hoofed animal.

"This looks like a large CAT track." said Fortier to himself.

Those at the Fort told strange and scary stories about over grown cats that hunt anything in their paths, stories they heard from the Aboriginals near the St. Lawrence River. Fortier quickly starts to track the cat, Fortier stands and looks out onto the lake and can see the path it took across the lake to the shoreline; and then into the trees.

"It's headed back toward our camp." claimed Fortier as he quickly mounted his horse and gave the horse a kick to hurry back to where the men were making camp.

The horse traveled in a quick canter, back along the path it had cut in the snow along the trees.

"MAKE... A... LARGE... FIRE... HURRY!" yelled Fortier as

RICHARD HERRON

he was just close enough for the men to hear him.

"OK!" yelled Antin in response, as Antin would never question what Fortier had him do… he just did it.

"Hurry men we need to make this a big fire quickly." said Antin in a nervous voice, because he knew that there had to be a reason; and it couldn't be a good one.

The men added more dried leaves, pine needles, small twigs, and large blocks of wood to the small fire they had already set. Fortier arrives and quickly gets down from his horse and wraps its reins around a tree.

"Fortier what's wrong?" asked Antin.

"Quiet men." whispered Fortier as he rushes past the men to the other side of the fire carrying his gun, now looking deep into the forest; scanning slowly; high and low for any sign of a large cat.

Complete silence had now consumed their camp, no one dared to move; no one dared to speak; the men just started staring into the shadows of the forest just like Fortier was doing. Watching the shadows flicker with the fires light, fear now filled the camp; none of the men knew what lurked in the forest. They were so scared that they didn't want to know what was wrong now, there was no sound other than the crackle of the fires burn.

"You have your guns?" whispered Fortier as he stared into the forest.

"Yes." whispered Antin as he slowly reached over and picked it up from where it was leaning against the tree.

"Is it loaded?" whispered Fortier as he pulled back the flint lock on his gun and slowly poured a little bit of gun powder, readying his musket for action.

"It is loaded sir." Antin whispered in response and just then… Fortier's slow movement of scanning the forest stopped.

Fortier's eyes locked onto a scary green set of eyes that flickered by the fires light, in the black darkness of the forests shadow. The creature that belonged to those eyes noticed Fortier's change in demeanor, the eyes backed a little and then a loud GROUL and HISS could be heard… the eyes then disappeared; and then with no warning;

"POW!" Fortier fired his gun into the air.

"TABRANACK!" swore Antin as he and the rest of the men hit the ground, only Fortier stood staring into the forest.

"Men, make sure this fire is well kept… and I want five other fires around our camp, make sure all of the guns are loaded and ready… we will be taking turns sleeping tonight, three at a time… we are being hunted men." said Fortier in a low calm and chilling voice.

"What was it?… do you think it's gone?" asked Demarr.

"The shot might have scared it off… but if it's hungry enough, it will be back; and we need to be alert and ready." said Fortier.

"It's a large cat, like the ones the Aboriginals speak about, the one they call Cougar… it's not some tall tale… one of them is out there hunting us, I seen its tracks heading back this way to our camp; very large paw prints; the size of my fist. At first light when the sun is high enough we will continue west, I seen Tarin's markers… if it's still hunting us, we will be able to see it coming in the daylight… that's if it doesn't come for us tonight." said Fortier with anxiety in his demeanor.

"Basile, Marc and I will take the first watch… the rest of you get some sleep if you can… I will try and figure out what we will do tomorrow." said Fortier.

The men ate some dry goods that didn't require cooking; they didn't want to further stir the Cougar's appetite. The men turned in for the night as the other three kept vigil and carefully watched the shadows.

Hunted   Day 2

    The sun can barely be seen as rolls of clouds have made their way in overnight, the sun sits low in the sky… it has barely risen. This morning has many new challenges for this party, patches of thick clouds have been snowing since the early hours of the morning; the wind has been blowing a chill on the men; waking those that were sleeping; all of the men have been awake a few hours before the sun had risen.

    "Kill that horse and spill its guts." ordered Fortier.

    "What? My horse… why?" said Basile confused at Fortier's orders.

    "We don't have the time to switch the supplies from horse to horse. You can ride one of the horses that are carrying our supplies, but you need to switch horses often; we don't want to wear out any of the horses to badly." replied Fortier.

    "I am hoping that the cougar will want to eat the dead horse and then leave us alone… Basile… please do as I ask." said Fortier in a solemn tone in his voice.

    "POW!" a gun shot rang out as the men were almost finished breaking camp and readying the horses, Basile had put down his horse. The men ride single file on their horses keeping a careful eye on the forest beside them… Tetu is the last in the line riding his horse seated backwards with his gun ready for any attack.

    The men are all hoping that the wind and snow will hide any trace of their scent away from the cougar, they slowly make their way back onto the lakes ice; a little ways off the shore; the party stops.

    "Let's stop here men… there is enough distance between us and the forest tree line, if that cat comes for us now… we have a

fighting chance. Make a fire and make breakfast, the chill in the air is going to consume a lot of our energy... we all need to eat. " said Fortier as the men were happy to agree.

A very large cougar stares down the steep hill deep inside the forest… it smells the fresh blood spilled out from the horse. Carefully the cougar makes its way down the hill with a hunger that controls all of its instincts. The cougar creeps toward the horses dead carcass… cautious and excited for all of the fresh meat left by the men; left by the men hoping for safe passage. The cougar starts tearing into the meat of the horse, its mouth painted with blood as it savers this morning's breakfast.

"POW!" the cougar jumps into the air and instinct takes over, and makes a run for its life but it's too late. The cougar falls over from the mortal wound it had received… it has fallen dead. From a very short distance from the horse, Basile gets up off the ground; removing his snow covered blanket that he was using to camouflage himself into the snow.

"MAKE ME KILL SABATIAN WILL YOU… CALISE TABRANAK… YOU SHOULD HAVE KNOWN BETTER THAN TO ATTACK THE FRENCH!" yelled Basile angrily and scared as his adrenaline rushed through his veins.

"FUCK that was scary!" claimed Basile as he dropped his gun, now trying to calm himself.

Fortier and the men are just starting to eat their breakfast.

"We will wait a little longer… if we don't see Basile soon we will head back and… oh… here he comes." said Fortier, Basile walking out from the forest toward the party.

Thick snow blowing across the lake as it pelts the men, Basile's shadowy out line appears through the blinding blizzard, his features grow clearer as he approaches.

"We were going to come get you soon... you were starting to worry me. " stated Fortier as he stood up.

"Come have some breakfast. " said Fortier as he started to make Basile a plate.

"Anyone interested in having Cougar for supper tonight? " asked Basile as the men now see why it took him so long to get to them as he was dragging the cougar on the snow using his blanket as a sled.

The men all gathered to have a look at the beast.

"CALISE... that thing is huge!" said Antin taking the words right out of everyone's mouths.

"I am going to skin him and hang him on my wall... make me kill Sabastian tabranak!" said Basile as he lightly kicked the cougars head.

"Hey, how would you want to cook it? " asked Demarr with a smiling smirk on his face.

"With an apple in its mouth... I'm going to roast him like a PIG!" yelled Basile with a smile now on his face, and all of the men burst into laughter.

"Alright now let's finish up breakfast and then get moving. " said Fortier with a smile on his face.

The men carried on with conversation about the details of the cougar kill and finished up their food. The rescue party continued pushing on through the snow storm until they finally reached the other side of the lake, they now had to search for another marker; hoping that they didn't miss any of them.

Dumont's Fate   Day Three

The snow storm seems to break a little, and the sun seems to beam a little more; it looks like the worst of this morning's blizzard has past. With all of the mornings cook ware stowed away, and the cougar wrapped up and tied to the back of one of the supply horses; the men mount their horses.

"Let's head to that tree line and find those markers." said Fortier as he led his men off the lakes ice.

He was now relieved to be past the lake hoping the travels ahead would be less eventful, fearing the worst and hoping for the best; Fortier just wants everyone to return alive. Travel seemed easier now that Mother Nature seemed to be cooperating, the wind died down no longer sending a chill to the bone. They now near the tree line which seems to wrap around the lake like a barrier.

"Over there… a marker." says Tetu as he points to the right of the parties current course.

Fortier looks at the direction Tetu was pointing,

"Alright, were not far off… let's get going." said Fortier while giving his horse encouragement.

The men shortly find themselves at the marker left by Tarin and his men, Fortier searches for the second marker for the direction.

"There it is… they headed straight into the forest here… the path they took looks good, lucky for us the hill looks not too steep… we should he able to ride the horses." said Fortier.

It was a large hillside covered in trees but the angle of the climb was gradual, which was a pleasant surprise. Onward the men took their time moving the horses up the easiest path

available. The sun now brightly bursting through the forest with its rays of comfort, birds now singing and dancing from tree to tree; two moose climbed the hill ahead of the men and rushed off at the site of the strangers; adding a cheerful mood to the men as they occupy the men's minds as they travel up the vast hillside. Making their way over downed tree trunks and some tight squeezes through the trees, the horses pushed forward as the men chatted amongst themselves to try and break the paths animosity.

"You know... just to say... I now proclaim these lands... Lands of Demarr!" stated Demarr with a proud tone to his voice.

The men all looked at each other curiously.

"Can you do that?" asked Basile with a puzzled look on his face.

"Of course I can... no one else from France has done it yet!" stated Demarr with pride in his voice; Basile quickly looked at Tetu with a smirk on his face.

"But why would you want to name these lands that?" asked Basile now smiling at Tetu, who in turn was now smiling back at him; waiting for what was to come next.

"I don't understand... what do you mean?" questioned Demarr who seemed confused to the question.

"Well... why would you want to name these lands after such a dumb shit that stinks of moldy clam-chow-dair... a man who farts so violently in his sleep that we had to put down my horse the next day to put it out of its MISERY!" said Basile laughing so hard that he barely got all of the words out of his mouth, all of the men stopped their horses they were laughing so hard.

"It hurts!" said Marc barely as he holds his stomach because his stomach muscles are so tight from the laughter that he is in pain, tears are starting to roll down his cheeks; Marc falls from his horse and now the men's laughter BURST even worse than before un able to contain themselves.

Demarr laughing hysterically quickly shouts,

"If I would have ate cabbage… hahahahaha… I could have finished him off!" laughed Demarr with tears now rolling down his face crouched over his horse.

The men all laugh uncontrollably, all in pain and tears flow from their eyes; Fortier can barely muster out any words.

"Stop hahahaha stop hahahaha it hurts!" said Fortier laughing hysterically, the men dare not say anymore because of the pain of the laughter; as Tetu now falls from his horse.

Painfully the laughter continues with each man trying to stop, and then they all hear a loud *"GRRRRRrrrr!"* the laughter quickly stops and the men all look up and see a mid-sized grizzly bear. It looked to be a young bear about three years old; it was just a little ways off in the distance to the right of the parties path.

"Demarr… NOW!… let him have it… fart in its direction… now's your chance to kill him!" said Basile as he burst out laughing again, then all the men started laughing as they pictured Demarr farting in the bears direction.

"OK… but there might be collateral damage." laughed Demarr.

Fortier who was the only one not laughing *"POW!"* fired a shot into the air and the bear ran off further into the forest out of site.

The men's laughter calmed down as they watched the bear run away.

"Ok, let's get to the top of this hill and see what the rest of the day has instore for us." stated Fortier as he and the men began to continue the assent up to the top of the hill.

The rest of the climb seemed to go by quickly as the men had a lot to occupy their minds, the mornings events played out in their

heads; keeping the parties spirits up in spite of the long trek ahead. Fortier reaches the top and looks at the view ahead. With a light breeze blowing and the sun now lighting the landscape, Fortier sees that the forest ends soon and a large land mass of plains.

"Won't be long now men... we will be on flat terrain soon." said Fortier assuring the men that the trek should get easier.

The men slowly make their way through the trees and finally reach the tree line, but Fortier spots something odd.

"Out there... just on that small hill... do you see it Antin?" asked Fortier confused as to what he was seeing.

"Antin, you and I will go have a look... the rest of you should prepare lunch; we will be back shortly." said Fortier as he and Antin started off toward the hill.

They were now about half way to the odd structure.

"What do you think it is?" asked Antin with a very puzzled look on his face.

"I do not know... but I hope it's not Aboriginal in nature." stated Fortier.

The men stopped at the bottom of the hill and stared at the small structure, they were looking at many long tree limbs and twigs bent and folded over each other making what looked like a small door less tent.

"Wait here I will go have a look." said Fortier as he climbed down from his horse.

Fortier slowly made his way up the small hill, looking around to see if he could spot any signs of indigenous peoples watching him but he could see none. He reached the structure, there were no aboriginal feathers or skulls on the structure; so Fortier bent down and peered through one of the gaps in the sticks.

"...shit..." said Fortier quietly to himself as he pulled himself away from the structure.

Fortier took off his hat and quietly said a short prayer, Antin seen Fortier remove his hat and lower his head… Antin did the same knowing this couldn't be good.

"Antin… it's Dumont." said Fortier as he started walking down the hill.

"I recognize the beaded pattern on his jacket." said Fortier with a solemn look on his face.

"Tarin and Andre must have built this tomb for him… the ground is to frozen to properly burry a man out here… this would be the best they could do for him." said Fortier as he looked into Antin's face.

"Yes… yes it would be, what do you think happened?" asked Antin.

"I would rather not say." said Fortier with a now Grave look on his face.

"Let's head back to the men." said Fortier, and they started back to where the men were finished making lunch.

"What is it?" asked Tetu as Fortier and Antin had arrived at the makeshift camp.

"I am sorry to say… it is Dumont." said Fortier gravely as the men's expressions turn somber.

"What do you think happened?" asked Basile quietly looking at the hill where Dumont's body was laid to rest.

"I didn't want to say… but it looks like he had a run in with a carnivore… maybe a bear… but I am thinking it was that cougar… animals are territorial, and that cougar clearly owned this area." said Fortier as the men looked saddened.

"We will set up camp here… we could all use some rest." said Fortier in light of the bad news they all had just received.

Basile yanked the wrapped up cougar off the back of the horse and it hit the snow covered ground with a loud thud.

"What are you doing?" asked Demarr.

"In Dumont's honour I am going to pre-pare this cougar for tonight's dinner." said Basile as he started to skin and gut the cougar.

"I will roast him like a pig... but... the apple is going in its ASS! CALISE TABRANAK!" said Basile with anger in his voice.

"But wait!" said Demarr quickly.

"What?" replied Basile.

"Well then who gets the apple?" said Demarr with a smirk on his face as he and Basile's eye's locked; Basile's face of anger slowly changed to almost a grin.

"It's ALL YOURS DEMARR!" laughed Basile who was quickly followed by all of the men.

"Bon Appetite!" replied Demarr as he laughed.

Demarr and Basile have always been best of friends, they grew up together and have been there for each other... like brothers. When either one sees the other is sad or in a bad mood, they like to cheer each other up. They have a very light hearted demeanour, and conquer all their hard times with a laugh; always trying to out wit each other and all those around them certainly enjoy their jokes and their company. The men on this rescue mission really appreciate Demarr and Basile, because they are very good spirits that help the men get through each day with their wonderful personalities; no matter what the situation is they know they need to be there for one another... brothers.

Everyone is settled warmly by the campfire, the night stars shine and twinkle forever in the sky; the snow covered ground acts as the earths lamp of light as it captures the glow of the nights moon. The crackle of the fire shares a little more light for the men as they finish this night's dinner.

"Hey Basile... can you pass the salt... and some more cougar!" laughed Demarr as he showed his empty plate to Basile.

"You must wait your turn, I have not yet finished my second plate yet; and you are now on your fourth you bastard!" giggled Basile as he showed his plate was almost cleaned of food.

"Basile, your cougar tastes fantastic... what is your secret?" poked Fortier hoping to stir the pot even further for a laugh.

"I will tell you nothing the secret is miiinnneee... as I am the GREATEST FRENCH COUGAR CHEF that has ever lived... no other Chef can tame the meat of a cougar like me... I call this delicacy, this quizine, this fine piece of poultry art... FELINE DARRY-AIRE!" said Basile as he lifted his hand gently into the air and looked up into the night's sky; and all of the men roared with laughter.

The men settle down and continue to finish their plates; Basile and Demarr help themselves to more cougar meat.

"Fortier, sir." said Tetu showing a bit of concern on his face as he looked at the fire.

"Yes Tetu." replied Fortier as he turned his attention to Tetu, seeing that something was on his mind.

"What do you think has become of Tarin and Andre... would they keep going?... or would they have turned back? What do you think?" asked Tetu knowing he had put a damper in the mood, but he wanted to know what his leader thought.

"I understand your concerns, I think those questions are probably going through everyone's heads; I have been thinking about how much further they would have or could have gone... they would have had enough supplies to continue." said Fortier, and without saying because of the loss of Dumont; they would now have ample supplies to continue.

"At this point would Tarin continue this journey... yes, he

would follow orders; my current plan is to travel the plains west and look for markers. We should find markers at least by noon tomorrow... I would think, if we don't we will need to have a discussion. " said Fortier assuring his men that this was his plan for the next day's search.

"Ok, thank you Fortier... I am just concerned now... that our efforts success look bleak. " continued Tetu now looking at Fortier, and as all the men are now looking at their leader eager to hear his response; hoping for reassurance of Tarin and Andre's survival.

"This is what I am thinking... from this point on, if they run into a bear... they will be fine just like us... but the chances of them running into another cougar is almost no chance of that happening... and wolves stay away from fires, and besides they have guns. " Fortier responded and paused for a moment, no longer looking at the men; he started to stare at the fire with concern in his face.

"But, I am concerned if they have met a new tribe... or if we meet a new tribe. " Fortier continued.

"Our voyages to the east coast, meeting the Aboriginal tribes have been successful... we are all friendly and trade with each other... but when meeting a new tribe it could be dangerous... fear of new peoples can cause dangerous events, fear can cause a man to kill; and if Tarin and Andre had met or if we meet a new tribe... they could be hostile out of fear. " said Fortier with a very distant look on his face as he stared at the fire.

"What do you want us to do if we run into a new tribe? " asked Tetu.

"Stop your horses... and don't make any sudden movements, if they approach us; stay on your horse and don't make a sound... I will try to deal with the situation. " said Fortier.

"How will we know if they are hostile? Shouldn't we draw

our guns just in case?" asked Tetu.

"If they are hostile... you for sure won't have a chance to draw your guns... we will already be dead... and none of us will have even seen any of them... the aboriginals hunt with their bows, they ambush their prey from hiding... their prey never even knows what has killed them." stated Fortier as the men all now stare at the fire with a grave mood in the air.

"That's why I told all of you not to bother looking for them back at the burial grounds... we really have no chance of survival against hostiles... all we can do is be respectful and show no aggression...or we are dead." said Fortier bringing the dangers of this journey into light for his men.

All the men were letting the moment sink in and remembering all of Fortier's advice… never to forget his orders. The men sat quietly for some time staring at the fire thinking about the rest of the journey ahead, thinking about Tarin and Andre's fate; and hoping they are still alive.

"Demarr... did you have enough cabbage tonight, there is some left if you are still hungry." asked Basile in a very quiet and soothing tone,

"Yes thank you... but I will finish it off, I wouldn't want it to go to waste." replied Demarr in a kind manner as he got up to help himself to the last of the cabbage.

"Well that's it!" said Basile angrily,

"If those hostile Tribes are following us tomorrow... they are DEAD, DEMARR WILL BE FARTING THROUGHOUT THE DAY... THEY WILL HAVE NO CHANCE OF A SNEAK ATTACK; HE WILL BE ON THE VERGE OF EXPLOSIVE FLATULENCE... ALL DAY... some will be silent... and deadly... they will not know what killed them." laughed Basile and all of the men laughing with Basile hysterically; Demarr had to sit back down because he was

laughing too hard.

"FFFFIIIRRRRT" Demarr accidently farted as he sat, Basile screamed through all of the laughter;

"WERE ALL GONNA DIE!" the laughter turned into crippling laughter as the men could do nothing to stop it, all they could do is lay there laughing until it stopped.

The laughter had finally stopped and the men all did their nightly chores and got ready for bed, with the fire fed with more logs; the men were ready for a warm night's sleep.

A Wailing Heart   Day four

Fortier wakes and breakfast is already cooking.

"Antin, that coffee wouldn't be ready would it?" asked Fortier.

"Yes it is, help yourself." said Antin with a smile; Fortier made himself a coffee and took a sip quietly looking around and enjoying the birds playful morning antics.

"Breakfast is ready." declares Antin, the men all gather and help themselves to the bacon, eggs, and the morning coffee.

"Thank you Antin." said Marc as he fills his plate.

"You are very welcome Marc" replied Antin.

Antin and Marc are very good friends, Antin knows that Marc is very quiet and doesn't say much so when Marc says something… it's rare; and Antin makes sure to respond to him… because it is a chance for Antin to show that he appreciates Marc's company. Marc is a quiet and humble man, he is best known for his size and strength; a beast of a man but very kind… he was always willing to help and never strayed from a hard day's work; a man of honour… and he wore it on his sleeve. The men finish their breakfast and clean up the dishes and break camp.

Fortier and his men climb on to their horses and start off going directly west with the sun on their backs, the day is bright with no clouds in the sky; today feels like a warmer day with barely a breeze blowing; they start to make their way onto the open plains. There are small bundles of trees and bushes scattered throughout the environment, small rolling hills are spread out across the prairie.

"We are going to make our way to that small mound of trees over there to see if we can find any markers." explained Fortier as

he pointed to the small patch of trees a little ways ahead.

"Look there." said Tetu as he pointed at a red fox playing in the distance, running and playing in circles; in and around some small bushes; jumping and running; the fox finally settles down and sits to have a rest; the playful antics captivate the men's attention as their horses slowly walk through the snow.

The men smile and watch as the fox starts to hunt. The fox walks out into the field, slowly with her ears poised up and listening for the smallest sound under the snow. The fox stops suddenly staring at the snow, the fox rears up onto its back legs and jumps into the air; and drives her face into the snow burying her face in the snow up to her ears. She removes her head from the snow with a small mouse in her clenched teeth, after she finishes her snack; she is off running and playing and moving on with her day; off into the distance the fox disappears.

"Fortier, why didn't you shoot the fox?" asked young Tetu curiously.

"What... Little Red... we don't need meat, we have enough; and we don't need pelts; we only take what we need from these lands and Little Red is too beautiful to shoot... what we need is to find a.... marker and there it is!" said Fortier with a bit of excitement and relief in his voice.

The men reach the marker and search for the second; they find the second that points in the direction they need to go.

"Looks like they headed north west... must be headed toward that large hill of trees over there, alright let's go." said Fortier as he gave his horse a small kick and a tug on the reins and off they all went with a new direction, no longer feeling lost; the men were happy to have found the markers because it gave the men hope that Tarin and Andre were still alive.

The horses are kicked into a slow canter across the seemingly never ending fields, they are close to reaching the large hill of trees… and then Fortier spots something that stops him dead in his tracks.

"EVERYONE STOP, WOOooooowww." yelled Fortier.

"Raise your hands and don't make a sound… don't make eye contact… let me try to deal with them… don't do anything… or you could kill us all." said Fortier.

From out of the trees… like ghost apparitions, galloping at full speed were fifteen painted horses; fierce stallions charging forward toward Fortier and his men; carrying fifteen painted Aboriginal Warriors yelling in battle cries and waving tomahawks in the air with a fearless stare in their eyes.

"Give me the horse with the cougar skin and the dried meat and stay here, if they kill me… defend yourselves." Fortier says.

With the one horse in tow Fortier gives his horse a short kick to make the horse walk forward, as the horse walks Fortier drops the horse reins and holds his hand high in the air showing no aggression to what seems to be certain death charging toward him. The warrior in the lead of the charge yells at his fellow tribe's men.

"Stop the spirit!" yelled the warrior and the other warriors break off from the forward charge leading left and right.

Bringing their horses to a stop about ten meters away from Fortier on either side of him, Fortier's horses are now standing still as he is surrounded on three sides. The lead warrior slows his stallion and slowly walks his horse to meet Fortier, the warriors on either side of Fortier are yelling fiercely at him. The lead warrior is staring violently into the eyes of Fortier. Fortier drops the reins of the horse in tow and he holds both hands in the air. The lead warrior stops his horse in front Fortier and the other warriors instantly go silent. The warrior looks Fortier over… within his angry stare; you can see he is confused by the color of his white skin. Fortier notices that the warrior has never seen a white man, Fortier slowly brings down his arm pulling back his sleeve exposing the skin on his arm and shows it to the warrior; the warrior slowly leans over and looks at Fortier's arm; at the pale white complexion and the brown hairs that cover his arm. The warrior slowly reaches over and touches the skin on the pale rider in front of him, then he sits back on his horse convinced it is not a spirit in front of him… just a strange looking man. Fortier slowly reaches into his chest pocket and pulls out a piece of dried meat and holds it out to the warrior in front of him, the warrior looks at Fortier and takes it from him… the warrior takes a bite and chews the meat. Fortier takes another piece from his pocket, his teeth tear the piece and he chews the piece dried meat; Fortier now shows a small smile to the warrior trying to show that he means no aggression. The warrior chews the meat and gives a simple nod of his head. Fortier waits for the warrior to finish the meat. Fortier, knowing that the warrior would not understand his words… Fortier points to the horse he has in tow; the warrior looks at the horse Fortier acknowledged; not understanding the gesture. Fortier raised both hands and slowly got off of his horse. Fortier walked over to the horse and opened up the wrapped up cougar skin and showed the warrior the cougar head. The warrior looked impressed with the cougar trophy and then he looked at his warriors who were watching Fortier carefully. Fortier covered the cougar skin back up and then opened a bag on the side of the horse, Fortier slowly reached in the bag and pulled out a handful of dried meat to show the warrior; who stared at Fortier curiously. Fortier put the meat back into the bag and closed it, Fortier then slowly picked up the horses reins; holding the reins up Fortier slowly walked toward the warrior offering him the horse, the meat,

and the cougar skin.

The warrior looked surprised and motioned NO with a swipe of his hand.

"NO!" said the warrior with a harsh stern voice.

He would not accept the cougar skin because it was not his trophy. The warrior took his reins of his stallion and walked his steed up to the horse Fortier was holding and knocked the bag that held the cougar skin off of the horse.   The warrior then walked his horse past the other horse and turned the horse around and stopped beside Fortier. The warrior looked at Fortier in the eyes and slowly took the reins of the horse Fortier was holding, the warrior then yanked a feather that was attached to his horses hair with a thin leather string and handed it to Fortier. Fortier took the feather and the warrior gave a short and almost un noticed nod… the warrior then kicked his horse and charged away from Fortier with the horse in tow.   The other warriors chased and joined their leader heading back to the tree line they came from, without a sound they disappeared back into the forest of trees.

Fortier looks back at his men, places his hands on the saddle of his horse.

"WE GET TO LIVE TODAY!" yelled Fortier to his men.

Fortier rests his head in relief against his saddle. The men kick their horses and race up to Fortier.

"I thought they were going to kill us all!" said Tetu with fear and disbelief on his face.

"I knew we had a chance to live… like I said before, if they wanted us dead; for sure… we would not know until it was too late; because they approached us head on I knew they were curious as to who we are. This was them seeing if we were bad spirits, they charged to see if we would charge back at them; meaning we were bad spirits; we didn't charge back so the lead

warrior stopped his warriors from killing us all. It is a good thing none of you panicked, just that gesture alone saved us all; they came with the intention to kill us all… but we gave them no reasons to follow through." said Fortier.

Fortier looked down at the feather in his hand; it was attached to a thin leather like string which was painted with blue and yellow dots.

"What is that?" asked Antin.

"I don't know… it was like he gave it to me in trade." said Fortier as he looked it over.

"What are you going to do with it?" asked Antin.

"Well… I think I am going to attach it to my horse's hair like he did… I think it looks nice." said Fortier as he tied it to his horse's hair.

"That does look nice." stated Demarr.

Basile gets off his horse and picks up the cougar skin package and ties it to the back of his saddle.

"Why didn't he want the cougar skin? It's a nice one!" stated Basile as Fortier gets back up onto his horse.

"I am not sure, Aboriginals have many customs and different traditions; these are not the same as the tribes in the east. These warriors look very different from them, to these warriors it might be a superstition to take someone else's animal kill; it might be a spiritual tradition." said Fortier only guessing as to the reason why the warrior did not want the cougar skin.

"Well I am glad he did not want it… she is going on my wall!" Basile stated with authority.

"I thought it was a male cougar?" questioned Demarr confused by Basile.

"It wassss… but I removed his gender berries and made him my bitch!… you see… SHE is going on my wall." boasted Basile as

Demarr and the other men all chuckled and laughed at Basile's reasoning.

The men followed Fortier to the tree line of the forest and found another set of markers,

"The markers point west following the tree line, so we have our direction... lets go." said Fortier as he readied his horse.

"Wait!" said Antin.

"We are on day four, if they were still alive we should have seen them by now? Wouldn't you think they would have been on their way back? We should have seen some sort of trace of them coming this way don't you think Fortier?" asked Antin in a bit of a panic, un sure if he… or they should proceed with the rescue.

"Yes you are right Antin; I know what you mean... I have been thinking the same thing since yesterday. The end of today will be the fourth day, it will be as far as they were to travel; we have not seen any trace of them heading back using the markers they set for themselves to get back. That does have me worried, but I have come to the conclusion that by the end of today; we will know the fate of our friends... good or bad news... we will know." stated Fortier with determination in his voice.

"But, if their fate was bad... I don't want to end up with the same fate." said Tetu with a very worried look on his face.

"If it was you... out there Tetu, I would do exactly what we are about to do... we are going to press on...; and find our friends... and save them if we can." said Fortier with pride and encouragement in his voice.

"Yes Fortier, you are right... I am sorry." replied Tetu.

"Don't be sorry Tetu, we are all thinking the same thing... I have never failed a task... and I am not going to start now. If there is u chance to rescue our friends... Tarin and Andre; I am willing to risk everything... because they would do the same for each of

us. " said Fortier, and the men all nodded in agreement with Fortier.

"Let's head out men, the day has not killed us yet... and the day has only begun... we will go and face this day head on. " said Fortier as he kicked the side of his horse, driving the horse into a heavy canter along the tree line... west.

The rescue party travel for some time, following the tree line that seemed to stretch across the plains endlessly for hours. They continued on following the markers set on the trees, left by Tarin. The men were growing tired, they were snacking on their dried meat as they travelled; not wanting to stop; wanting to reach their destination... hoping each marker was the last.

"OOOOOoooooooooooowwwwwwoooooooooooooooo. " was heard from inside the trees, from inside the dence thickly forest the men traveled beside.

"WOLVES!" yelled Demarr as all the horses stopped, and now a chorus of wolves started to sing their bone chilling song.

"It's a wolf pack, move out into open ground... get away from the tree line. " ordered Fortier as the men all followed his lead.

Three wolves tear out of the forest chasing the retreating men, riding as fast as their horses are willing to stride. They kick the horses driving them as fast as they can into the open ground.

"AAAHHHHHHHhhhhh!" someone yelled, and was heard over the clamoring of the horses stampeding hooves.

When they were a fair distance away from the trees, Fortier turned his horse and seen what looked to be fifteen huge wolves traveling at great speeds poised on their prey; Fortier grabbed for his rifle.

"SHOOT THEM!" Fortier ordered.

Fortier fired a shot and the men turned their horses and

stopped… and they all took aim. Shots rang out sounding like staggered cannon fire.

RICHARD HERRON

Three wolves seemed to be ripping and tearing at the snow, and then Fortier seen a man's arm flail up from the ravaging of the wolves.

"Oh no…" said Fortier quietly with great concern in his voice.

A few of the men had secondary rifles and they fired once more. Fortier has already reloaded his rifle and took careful aim at one of the three wolves ripping at one of his men, Fortier fires and hits one of the wolves and with a short yelp; the black wolf quickly falls to its death. The guns fire and a few injured wolves quickly retreat into the forest.

Fortier turns to his men, frantically he searches their faces to see who was missing……….

"Demarr?" said Fortier quietly with confusion and sadness in his face.

The men all stare back at Fortier then look at each other searching for Demarr.

"No… Demarr… DEMARR… NOOOO DEMARR!" screamed Basile as he kicked his horse riding back the way they came, now Basile was crying.

"DEMARR… DEMARR!" wailed Basile as he approached the lifeless body of his best friend.

Basile jumped from his horse and kneeled beside his fallen brother, picking him up and cradling his head as he wept so desperately for this not to be true.

"NOOOOooo Demarr Nooooo… please noooooo." cried Basile as he held his very best friend.

Completely crushed… Basile cried in agony. Fortier and the men all fought… not to shed a tear, trying to hide their sadness as they sat on their horses, staying away from Basile who wailed loudly in so much pain. Fortier and the men did not dare move from where they were, they waited hours until Basile had no more tears left to cry.

The men kept watch of the tree line with their rifles ready and built a fire out in the open, it was getting close to dusk. Fortier, with a heavy heart started to walk toward Basile, the men looked at Fortier and started to cook dinner; to have it ready for when the two returned. Fortier slowly approached Basile and put his hand on his shoulder, Basile exhausted from crying; sitting cold on the icy and snowy ground; breathing sadly with no energy left in his body.

"Basile... please come to the fire, we will take care of him." said Fortier in a very sad voice as he carefully did not look to see what had happened to Demarr. Deterring his eyes from looking at his lifeless body. Basile slowly and gently put Demarr's head onto the snowy ground and got up, Fortier and Basile slowly walked back to the makeshift camp. Tetu had cleared the snow and placed Basile's blankets beside the fire, with his saddle for a pillow.

"Basile... I prepared your bed... here is a plate of food for you, you need to eat before you go to bed... please eat." said Tetu.

Basile sat on his blankets by the fire and took the plate of food from Tetu. Basile was not hungry, he was filled with grief; but he ate anyway because he knew Tetu was right; he needed to eat.

Fortier motioned to the men to come to him.

"Antin and Marc, please gather some wood from the tree line for the fire... and for Demarr's burial. Tetu, please go with them and keep watch for the wolves; all of you bring your rifles. I'm going to stay here at the camp with my rifles and watch to make sure no wolves circle around and go for Demarr's body. I think we killed their Alpha, so I don't think they will return. Don't touch any of the dead wolves, if you leave your scent on them; and they

return with a new Alpha; they may track us for revenge... so don't go near them. " said Fortier quietly.

"Yes Victor... we will have it done as soon as we can... right away. " replied Antin with a great sadness. Antin rarely used Fortier's first name, he only used his first name when he wanted to show he was talking to his dear friend; a friend he admired.

The men did as they were asked, they collected all the wood needed. Basile had fallen asleep and all the men had went to collect Demarr's Body and brought him to their camp. Tetu was made to keep watch for any wolves return while the men built a sturdy tomb, made of wood for Demarr's body to rest peacefully; the wolves did not return this night.

Don't Go In There   Day Five

Fortier woke as the sun was just rising. Antin was already making breakfast for everyone, the smell of bacon, eggs, and fresh coffee filled the frosty air.

"You're up. " said Fortier quietly.

"I woke up two hours ago... I sent Tetu to bed from his wolf watch. I couldn't sleep any more, I figured it's time to cook up a large breakfast for everyone; no one ate too much last night. " said Antin quietly as he flipped the bacon in the pan.

"Thank you Antin. " said Fortier as he made himself a coffee.

"I will wake the men, breakfast is ready. " said Antin.

Antin woke the men for breakfast. They all woke hungry, it was a long night of night watch as the men took turns; all except Basile; the men let him sleep hoping the rest would help sooth some of his sorrow. Not many words were shared by the men, all were still grieving the loss of Demarr. The men all finished their food and each cleaned their dishes and broke camp. With their horses packed up, everyone was ready to go and they climbed onto their horses.

"It is with pain in our hearts... we need to press on with our rescue mission... Tarin and Andre are still out there, we need to find them... they need us... we are their only hope; and I don't want to fail them... let us take a moment of silence and pray for our very good friend Demarr. " said Fortier as he bowed his head, the men all removed their hats and silently prayed for Demarr.

The morning was quiet as the sun started to rise. The shadows started to stretch casting long outlines of trees across the snow covered terrain. Birds are just starting to chirp and start their day along with these men, giving the men something to listen to

and preoccupy their minds. The sky was clear with a few small white clouds slowly changing shape in the sky as the men road their horses single file in silence.

"The markers point to that forest off in the distance, it looks like we may be heading back into the trees gentlemen" said Fortier as he pointed at the large forest of trees that painted the scenery with its dark silhouette.

They slowly travelled across the plains taking hours to reach the forest. As they approached the forest the men studied the trees as the got closer. The trees somehow didn't look right, they looked large; old and ancient; and looked creepy to the point of unwelcoming. The tree line looked like a wall that was grown to keep people out, for miles and miles in either direction; North and South; the forest wall stretched across the lands; looking to warn all travelers to turn back and leave this place. Fortier stopped his horse about thirty yards from the tree line, and so did his men. Everyone stared at the trees, they went as far as the eye could see; very much like a wall; a wall that gave the men a very unsettling feeling through their flesh; to their very bones. Fortier looked for a marker and in fact found both, they marked the direction that lead strait into the forest.

Fortier and the men sat in their saddles for what seemed like minutes in silence.

"Does anyone else hear that?" asked Fortier quietly, the men all listened carefully… and quietly.

"I don't hear anything?" replied Antin quietly as he looked at the forest.

"Exactly, absolute silence… not a bird can be heard; I can't even hear a light breeze in the air." said Fortier with a very disturbed look on his face.

"I don't want to go in there… something isn't right." said

Marc with a hint of fear in his voice, but no one would say anything about it; or ask why he sounded afraid because they all knew; they were all thinking and feeling the same thing.

They sat and waited, and stared into the forest; listening for anything; listening for something; but... there was nothing. The large twisted trees in front of them seemed more and more foreboding as the minutes went by. The horses made whiny sounds and stomped the ground, they seemed unsteady.

"I don't think the horses want to go in there either." said Tetu.

"Something has them spooked." replied Antin as he stroked his horse's neck to try and calm the beast.

"I don't like this either... but Tarin and Andre are in there... they have marked the path... we need to go in... we must go in." stated Fortier, sounding as though he was not only trying to convince the men; but was also trying to convince himself as well.

Fortier gave his horse a short kick in the side and started into the forest... and the men he was leading; all reluctantly followed.

Once inside this strange forest... the men searched the woods with their eyes, like a child in a dark hallway; fearing what they cannot see; fearing what could be hiding... they could feel it. The sound of the horse's hooves crushing the thick snow, the sound was dampened by the surrounding large trees; making the sound of the crunching steps seem to mute out quickly. The horses breaths seem labored and loud like they were scared or in fear, and yet they carried on into the forest; doing their masters will. They push their way into the forest with hesitation like unknown forces were warning them off, all of their senses are telling them to turn back; but they can't... they need to find their friends. Deeper and deeper into the forest this rescue party continues, fighting all their instincts to turn back; they won't turn back.

"Can you feel that? What is that? This doesn't feel right! Everything is telling me to turn back!" yelled young Tetu.

"There is a meadow up ahead... let's keep going! Keep your wits about you, don't listen to your feelings!" yelled Fortier.

All of the men were feeling the same strange feelings, the horses were beginning to be hard to control; a struggle against some horrible unknown force... was it some kind of black magic or curse put upon the forest... and then... it stopped. Just as the rescue party entered the meadow... the strange force vanished.

"Look! That's impossible!" said Fortier.

They entered a very large circular meadow, but something mystical was in this meadow; this meadow was enchanted by some unknown force. Bright green trees and grass covered this meadow, the trees look very different than the ones in the forest; they looked twisted and very sick; there wasn't one spec of snow in this place of wonder. In the middle of this meadow was a single tee-pee. An aboriginal family could be seen, a mother stretching an animal hide; a painted warrior husband tending the fire wood; and a little boy running around playing with a stick. The men all stopped moving, there was nowhere to go; they didn't want to re-enter the forest. Then the warrior noticed the men and quickly stood up... and just stared at the men. The mother notices and quickly calls to her son.

"Little Fire" said the boy's mother, the boy stops and looks at his mother and sees she is staring into the distance; the boy looks to where she is looking and sees the men; he quickly runs to his mother and hides behind her.

The warrior points to the tee-pee and the mother rushes her son into the tee-pee and they disappear.

"Men, don't move... they look like they feel threatened. This

is a bad situation, don't underestimate the warrior; he has the upper hand. I am going to slowly walk up to him alone… if he kills me, turn back into the forest and head back to Jacques and tell him not to return to this area… leave this forbidden place." said Fortier quietly as he slowly got down from his horse.

None of the men answered, they wanted to stay quiet and very still. Fortier slowly lifted one of his hands and slowly started to walk his horse toward the warrior. Fortier got half way to the warrior's camp, and the warrior retrieved his tomahawk from the loop at his side. Fortier stops immediately and raises his hand higher into the air and shakes his head.
"NO!" yelled Fortier hoping the warrior would understand the meaning of his actions.
The warrior stood still and lowered the tomahawk but did not move. Fortier slowly started to continue to walk toward the warrior, being very careful of his movements. Fortier got about thirty feet from the warriors camp, and with his hands raised in the air; Fortier slowly sat onto the ground hoping the aboriginal warrior that stood in front of him would not just throw that tomahawk and kill him dead.

The warrior stood his ground, just staring at Fortier; confused and weary of this trespasser. Then, something caught the warrior's eye… the feather that hung from the mane of Fortier's horse. The warrior took a few slow steps forward and looked hard at the feather; the warrior pointed at the feather with his tomahawk and spoke.
"You have seen my brother." said the warrior.
"I was given this by another warrior." stated Fortier knowing that his words meant nothing to the warrior, as did the

warrior's words to Fortier.

"Star, come… they met Big Bear, he let them live." said the warrior who now put the tomahawk back into the loop at his side.

Star and her son Little Fire slowly exit the tee-pee, still showing signs of fear.

"Come, sit by the fire." said the warrior as he motioned to the fire.

Fortier understood what the warrior wanted, he slowly got up; let go of the horses reins; and slowly walked to the fire and sat down again. The warrior joined Fortier by the fire and sat down across from him. Fortier didn't know how to start the conversation so he waited. The warrior looked at Fortier… after a few moments the warrior looked at his wife.

"They must be looking for the two white men." said the warrior instinctively.

"Show them the way… make them leave." said Star as she was holding Little Fire close to her.

"If I do, they will die." said the warrior.

"Great Eagle, those other men did not listen to you; and neither will these men; just show them the way." stated Star.

"I must try to stop them from following the other two strange men, they don't know what lies past this place." said Great Eagle worried about the situation.

Great Eagle turned his head to Fortier and looked into his eyes… and waited.

"We are looking for two men, with white skin; have you seen them?" asked Fortier as he pointed at his skin on his arm.

"He pointed at his skin… he is looking for the others." said Star with absolution in her voice.

Great Eagle thinking Star was right, waved his hand with a slow motion; telling her to stop. Great Eagle then turned his attention back to Fortier.

"The two men went there." said Great Eagle as he pointed at what looked like an entrance, an entrance of two trees covered with animal bones; an entrance to warn off those who wish to enter.

Fortier looked at the entrance to the path Tarin and Andre had taken, and to Fortier… it did not look inviting. Fortier stood up and called to his men,

"We have the direction of where Tarin and Andre went, ride here very slowly." said Fortier as he didn't want to seem threatening to this family.

Great Eagle walked over to the entrance, waiting for the strange men to arrive. Fortier waited for his men and then he climbed onto his horse. In a single file they all slowly approached the entrance.

"Stop, don't go in there; I must try to warn you… this part of the forest is sacred to the spirits; it is the spirit world; don't follow the other two men." pleaded Great Eagle as he lifted both hands up trying to warn them off.

"Victor… he is definitely trying to tell us not to go that way." said Antin with concern in his voice.

"I know… and he isn't threatening us… he is trying to help us… but Tarin and Andre went in there… we need to continue." said Fortier as he looked into the eyes of Great Eagle.

"We must go… we have no choice… we have to save our friends." said Fortier as he pointed into the forest through the entrance trees that were covered in skulls and bones.

"Go then… I am to warn… not to interfere… may the spirits protect you." said Great Eagle as he lowered his hands and stepped aside. Fortier looked back at his men and then looked at Great Eagle,

"Thank you." said Fortier who then tore the hanging feather

from his horses mane and handed it to Great Eagle; Great Eagle took it from Fortier's hand.

Great Eagle understood the gesture and reached for a thin leather string that was around his neck, attached to it was a small medicine bag.

"For protection." said Great Eagle as he handed it to Fortier.

Fortier, not knowing the meaning; took kindly to the gesture and tied the medicine bag around his neck. Great Eagle then slowly motioned for the men to pass through the entrance, but with guilt and hope… he reluctantly let them pass. The men, single file… all pass through the entrance and into the forest. Star and Little Fire walked over to Great Eagle. Great Eagle puts his arm around Star and holds her firmly around her shoulder.

"You are the watcher of this forest… not of men… you did all that you could do." said Star as she watched the strange men carry on through the path.

"I know… that place is where the spirits walk… not a place for men." replied Great Eagle as he watched the men until they disappeared… from site; into the forest.

Great Eagle and his family turned and walked back to their home in the middle of the meadow.

The men travel for some time into the forest, something is different; the men don't have an over whelming feeling to leave the forest; they now have a calm reassuring feeling. Nothing is bothering Fortier, but there still is no sound among the twisted ugly trees; not a sound… only the steps of the horses hooves in the snow.

"There, that must be where Tarin Made camp… let's make camp there for the night; we have all had enough for today." said Fortier as he stopped his horse at the site where Tarin's camp fire was once lit.

RICHARD HERRON

The men made camp and readied the night's supper. Fortier and the men sat quietly and ate their food.

"Fortier, why do you think that warrior was trying to stop us from entering this forest?" asked Tetu.

"There is something wrong in here… we can all feel it… I don't know what it is Tetu… but we need to find Tarin and Andre and get out of here… something is very wrong with this place." said Fortier as he looked around at the forest that surrounded them, feeling worried and anxious; Fortier could only hope to find Antin and Andre soon.

The men all settled in and had their supper. None of the men were happy about having to continue with this rescue, but they all knew that they had to continue; for Tarin… and Andre… they would have done the same for them. Soon after supper all of the men went to sleep, all but one.

"I will take first watch tonight… I will wake you up in four hours Marc." said Antin as he readied three rifles for any dangers that may be hiding in the shadows of the night, and all the other men… went… to sleep.

Antin sat near the fire, stirring the newly made pot of coffee as he was looking out into the forest. It was quiet like every night, but he knew this forest was strange; because it was quiet all day as well. The flicker of the fire struck the trees of the forest providing very little light. The crescent moon sat lonely in the sky, very little glow struck the snow on the ground in the black of night. The trees twisted branches seemed menacing, like something out of a scary story parents would tell to their children; only Antin… was sitting in the middle of the scary story; only this was no story; this was real.

"What was that?" said Antin quietly.

Antin sat up more alert; his eyes widen trying to see through

RICHARD HERRON

the darkness. He thought he seen something large move from the corner of his eye, he thought he seen a lot of dark hair; but he could not be sure. He sat in silence staring into the forest searching for any movement; any sign of anything in the shadows. He sat silent… he did not move, only slowly turning his head slowly sweeping the forest with his eyes in absolute fear. After what seemed to be a long time had passed with no other movements, Antin started to relax.

"Must have been the flicker of the fire… uhhh." sighed Antin as he made himself a new coffee.

Antin trying to calm himself and trying to forget what he saw, passing it off as a shadow moving because of the flicker of the fire; trying to get back to normal as he tried to flush the fear from his mind. Hours pass… Antin now calmly sat and whittled a twig to pass the time; it was now time to wake Marc up for his turn.

"Marc… hey Marc it's your turn to watch." said Antin as he gave Marc a few short little shakes of his shoulder.

"What, oh… yes I am up." replied Marc as he slowly sat up.

"There is fresh coffee for you Marc." said Antin quietly with a smile.

"That sounds great, thank you Antin." said Marc as he got up and folded his blanket.

Antin laid down with his head on his saddle, and pulled his blanket over himself. Marc sat on a stump of wood by the fire.

"Good night Antin." said Marc quietly.

"Good night." said Antin quietly as he closed his eyes and fell quickly to sleep.

RICHARD HERRON

Follow The Tracks   Day Six

The sun is just starting to rise and lights up the forest's twisted trees, but something isn't right this morning.

"Where is he? Where is Marc? MARC! MARC!" yelled Tetu as loud as he could.

Fortier and the rest of the men woke, confused and concerned.

"Tetu, what's wrong?" asked Fortier with panic in his voice.

"Marc isn't here, he is missing!" replied Tetu.

"Could he be gone on a bathroom break?" asked Fortier.

"I thought that at first, but the fire is almost cold and the coffee is cold; Marc wouldn't let the fire go out." stated Tetu with great concern.

"MARC!... MARC!... MARC!" yelled Fortier as loud as he could, but there was no answer; as all the men stood in silence.

"Look for his tracks in the snow." said Antin quickly as he dashed off to the direction he thought he had seen something in the forest last night.

"Everyone slowly start searching for tracks in the snow." directed Fortier as everyone started scowering the snowy ground.

"STOP!... EVERYONE!... DON'T MOVE!" yelled Antin as he stared at the ground behind a tree.

Everyone stopped in their tracks and stared over at Antin.

"VICTOR!... COME OVER HERE, QUICK!" shouted Antin.

"What's the matter?" said Fortier as he hurried over to Antin.   Fortier reached Antin at the tree and looked down at what Antin was staring at, it was a HUGE set of foot prints; Fortier's mouth dropped open and could do nothing but stare.

"This is my fault." stated Antin with disbelief in his voice.

"Early last night... on my shift, I thought I seen something; I

thought the fire and the shadows were playing tricks on my eyes. I thought it couldn't be real, there was no noise... it had to be just my eyes playing tricks on me." said Antin as he was staring at the very large foot prints.

"What was it... what did you see?" asked Fortier with great concern.

"I was looking into the forest through the flicker of the fire, scanning for wolves or cougars; and in only a second... one second I thought I seen something large with long hair disappear behind a tree in this area... and there is the foot print. This is my fault... even if I thought it was not real, I should have told Marc about it; but I didn't think it was real. I only thought I seen hair hanging down in strands, this was no bear and I knew it wasn't because it would have come out to our camp. My eyes were just playing tricks on me... what I saw could have been the shoulder of an arm... at about seven feet high... which would make this thing eight or nine feet tall. It made no sense in my mind... it could not be real!" said Antin helplessly.

"This... THING... is huge... whatever it is." said Fortier in almost disbelief.

"This is not your fault... I would have thought the same as you... Marc probably would have laughed at you anyway, you know how he is." said Fortier as he tried to console Antin.

"Men, we have found a giant set of foot prints in the snow behind this tree... Antin and I are going to trace the tracks from here. Slowly spread out in every direction from the campfire outwards, we need to follow the tracks to wherever they meet up with Marc's tracks." said Fortier and the men all slowly started their search.

Fortier and Antin started tracking the prints, they led away from the camp; hiding behind every tree it passes. The tracks then change direction going to the left, starting to circle the camp; again hiding behind every tree. Fortier and Antin were now nearing Tetu.

"I found large foot tracks in the snow here… Tabranak! These are ENORMOUS!" said Tetu with amazement in his voice.

"Wait there." said Fortier as he and Antin continued to trace the tracks which were heading to where Tetu was standing.

The tracks met to where Tetu was standing, the three men were now walking together following the tracks in the snow.

"Over here… I found where the tracks meet." said Basile.

"Stay there." said Fortier as he and the other men continued to follow the tracks in the snow.

The tracks circled the camp, about three quarters the way around; and then moved diagonally into the forest; seemingly to be tracking Marc. These large tracks were now heading to where Basile was standing; the large tracks did in fact meet where Basile was standing.

"We are about fifty feet from camp, why would Marc be this far away from the camp?" wondered Basile.

"I don't think he would go this far for a bathroom break… I think he heard or saw something that caught his attention, and drew Marc out here; their tracks meet here." stated Antin.

"But where did Marc's tracks go?" asked Basile as he pointed to where Marc's tracks just disappear.

"The creature must be carrying Marc." guessed Antin.

"There is no blood… which means he could still be alive, let's gather the horses and break camp and follow the tracks; we need to find him." said Fortier as he started back to camp.

The men all broke camp and headed in the direction of the big foot prints. The men carried on into the forest following the foot tracks, deeper and deeper into the forest; the men were as silent as the forest; their eyes searching the forest… for anything. As the hours passed by the men helplessly wondered about the condition of their good friend… where was Marc being carried too? Starting to lose hope the men pushed onward, hoping that they will reach their friend in time.

"What is that?" said Fortier in a very confused voice.

Fortier, looking to his left through the dense trees; he points to what looks like an opening on the side of a large hill; but can barely distinguish it through the forests walls of trees.

"We should go have a look." said Fortier as he turned his horse left and pushed his horse into the dense trees.

"But the tracks don't lead in that direction." said Antin as he pointed at the large tracks smashed into the snow ahead.

"It could be trying to trick us hoping we would miss this hole in the hill… we have to check to see." said Fortier as he pressed on through the trees.

Basile and Tetu looked at Antin, and Antin stared back at them… confused look dawned Antin's face. Antin then turned his horse and followed Fortier, Basile and Tetu eyes locked in silence.

"Ahhh come on." said Basile quietly to Tetu as he kicked his horse and turned it to follow Fortier and Antin.

Tetu reluctantly followed the men, turning his horse to follow. The horses trudge through the snow brushing the trees as they pass them, the horses start to feel uneasy as they near the large hole in the hill; like an entrance… the horses start to whinny and will go no further.

"The horses don't want to go any further." said Fortier as his horse started to rear up.

"We will tie them up here and walk the rest of the way, Basile stay with the horses." said Fortier as he got off his horse.

All of the men did as Fortier asked, Basile stayed to watch

the horses and the rest of the men followed Fortier for the short walk to the hole in the hill.

"What is that?" said Antin in a loud voice.

Fortier, Antin, and Tetu all stopped dead in their tracks… and stared in dead silence. The entrance was now in site, it was about six feet high and looked to be carved into the hill; but that wasn't what has the men stone silent. Just a few feet inside the cave entrance were two very old looking totems made of tree logs and many human skulls… bones, each made to look like a nightmare of a creature, a pair of contorted creatures that were made to face into the cave.

"What in the devil…" said Fortier as he broke the silence. *"Do we have to go in there?"* questioned Tetu with fear in his eyes as his complexion continued to grow more pale by the second. The men all again stood in silence, and all were questioning themselves; in their minds; as each of their minds were telling them… don't go in there.

"The totems seem to be facing into the cave… that doesn't make sense, wouldn't you face them outward to ward off anyone from entering un… unless… they were made to keep something in…" said Antin as a terrifying fear now sank into the men's skin, scaring them to the bone.

"Look, I don't want to go in either… but we need to be sure Marc is not in there… and what if Tarin and Andre are in there, maybe they made camp inside the cave?" said Fortier, as he himself was not believing the bullshit line he was feeding to his companions; but he knew they had to search the cave to be sure none of the men were somehow inside.

"You really think that they could be in there?" questioned Tetu as he thought why would anyone want to go into a cave dressed with human bones, the fear was now sending horrifying

images racing through Tetu's mind; scattering his thoughts.

"I really don't know Tetu... but we need to make sure." said Fortier as he lit his lantern and started to walk inside.

The men reluctantly followed Fortier into the cave with frightening thoughts racing through their minds. Could it be a bear den? Could it be a cougar den?... or were those totem's holding back a much stranger and much more terrifying beast.

Slowly... Fortier leads his men further into the cave, they walk cautiously; their eyes scour the rock walls and floors; searching the surfaces of anything the lanterns light touches. The men have been walking for three minutes; each minute that passes seems like an eternity.

"Wait!" whispered Fortier sharply, quickly throwing his hand back to stop his men.

The men stop, each frozen in fear; each careful not to move a muscle; each wondering what Fortier had seen in the light that they had not seen.

"The cave seems to slant downwards now... deeper into the ground... watch your footing... be careful..." whispered Fortier as he led the men down the slope of the cave floor.

Slowly the men make their way down the shaft, deeper into the hills belly. After a few minutes the passageway levelled out and the cave opened up into a large open chamber. What the men now see has them in shock. Mounds and mounds of skulls and bones, from animals of all walks of life that inhabit these lands; and hundreds of human remains can be seen scattered amongst the mounds of remains. Stalagmites and stalactites can also be seen staggered throughout the chambers cavity.

"There is NO WAY they are down here!" claimed Tetu in a whisper.

"You don't know that!" whispered Fortier as he tried to

reason with Tetu.

"Yes I do… because there is NO FUCKING WAY I would come down here and see this… and then make camp!" whispered Tetu in absolute fear as his eyes shot around the cave chamber.

Fortier looks past the bones and sees that there are two shaft entrances leading further into the caves caverns.

"Look… at the other side of the chamber, let's go." whispered Fortier as he started to make his way over the bones, trying to show no fear so that his men would follow; his men followed in fear and in protest… but they knew they had to follow Fortier… he was the only one that had… a lantern.

Over the bones the men made their way to the other side of the chamber, trying not to make much noise. The men finish the trek over the remains and arrive at the two shaft entrances.

"This might not sound like a good idea… but this shaft on the right has more bones scattered on the ground… I think we should follow this one!" whispered Fortier uneasily to his men.

"Sounds great… at this point, does it really matter?" explained Tetu as he let out a quiet and nervous laugh.

The men enter the right shaft as they follow Fortier's lead. Walking on the trail of bones as they sometimes crunch and crack under their feet. Flies start to fill the air as they make their way further down the shaft, and now a disgusting smell starts to immerse; attacking the men's senses with the pungent smell of rotting flesh.

"Cover your faces to block some of the smell!" said Antin and all of the men reached into their pockets and pulled out their face scarves that they used when they travel during a snow storm.

The scarves helped a little but less than they would like. Fortier picked up his lantern and continued to light the way, further into the cave they pressed on. Fortier now notices something a ways ahead and he stops the men.

"I see light up ahead… must be the end of the shaft, I don't know what could be causing the light so let's be quiet and slowly make our way there." whispered Fortier as he continued to lead the men towards the light.

Brighter and brighter seemed the light to be; as the men got closer to the shafts exit. Each man was now being extra careful with each step, trying not to disturb the bones on the shaft floor. The men reach the shaft exit and Fortier motions the men to crouch down as he himself crouches very low. Fortier places the lantern down just inside the shaft exit, and slowly leads the men behind some large boulders a few feet ahead.

"I can't see where the light is coming from, and what is that clanging sound?" whispered Tetu as his back hugged the boulder behind him.

"I will climb up and have a peek… wait here." whispered Antin as he was trying to show some courage to his friends, to display why he was Fortier's lead man.

"Alright, but only a quick peek and then come back down." whispered Fortier as he was trying not to act nervous.

Antin slowly stood up and placed his left hand in a crack on the boulder and placed his right foot on a smaller rock, he then slowly lifted himself up higher onto the boulder; only high enough for his eyes to just peek over; to see what there was to see.

Quickly Antin jumps down and his eyes are staring wide open, open so wide that his stare was frightening; a stare that looked like his eyes were screaming in terror; and his lips are tightly sealed shut; quivering without a sound; Antin does not scream and does not make a sound… whatever is over that boulders edge has him so scared that he dares not make a sound. Antin can do nothing but stare at the men, he looks to be screaming in terror on the inside of his body; but he is completely frozen in fear. The men have no words… they too are now afraid to speak, they too are now frozen in fear from the look on Antin's face; and now a single tear starts to fall down Antin's cheek as his lips now start to quiver uncontrollably. Tetu starts to rub Antin's shoulder out of fear and trying to calm him down… no one says anything, all they can do is stare at Antin. After five minutes of complete silence and staring at Antin in horror, Antin slowly lifts his hand and places it on Tetu's shoulder; Tetu stops rubbing Antin's shoulder; and now with the same terror expression on Antin's face; many tears now start to slide down Antin's face; and with his eyes bulging Antin locks eyes with Fortier; Antin fights with everything in his soul not to scream the words…

"Don't… look down there." whispered Antin, and now as if his body was screaming in terror; tears now started streaming down his cheeks but Antin did not make a sound. Fortier wanted to just leave and so did the men, the men now are staring at Fortier wondering what to do. Fortier locks eyes with the men, each in turn and then looks at the ground; and then lifts his head up once more.

"I don't want to look… I am terrified, but in that split second that Antin looked… I have to make sure that he didn't miss seeing Marc, Tarin, or Andre." whispered Fortier carefully.

"Don't!" whispered Antin even quieter than before as he shook his head to say no.

Fortier had no choice, he had to look. Fortier slowly stood up and placed his hand on the boulder and got a good foothold, he slowly lifted himself up onto the boulder; then slowly peeked over the boulders edge… Fortier could do nothing but stare.

Hundreds of two foot little people that were mostly naked except they dawned a fur loin cloth. Their faces were twisted and had very sunken face lines, long and very hoarse eyebrows hang from their brows; sharp carnivorous teeth that looked able to clean any bone free of flesh; they each had an over sized nose and ears. Their bodies were disproportioned with very large heads with very little hair, and short muscular legs. Their arms were thin with large forearms and hands, hands that carry four fingers with no thumb. The large and vast chamber was a city of dwellings made of bones and gold, the dwellings lined the sides of the chamber that could only be explained as homes piled on top of one another; with ladders of bones that reach the chamber floor. A staircase of bones leads to the top of the caves chamber, to a walk way to the center of the chambers ceiling; where five giant uncut diamonds hang suspended where a fire is kept to light the diamonds which throws light to fill the chamber. At the cities center is a large gold smelting area, tons of gold ore rocks are piled high; six dwarfs can be seem feeding a large smelting cauldron; which then spills into a second hot cauldron. Two dwarfs can be seen collecting the spilling gold that pours from a human skulls mouth, the back of the skull is fastened to the side of the cauldron. They collect the spilling gold with hundreds of clay bowls. A very long line of dwarfs standing still, pass the gold filled bowls down the line passing the bowls hand to hand. The line of dwarfs stretches from this large chamber into another large chamber which can be seen. The gold filled bowls are passed through a huge entrance gate of animal bones that were covered in gold, making this entrance very eerie and yet grand. The line of dwarfs extends to the center of the chamber, where thick giant walls made of thousands of these gold bowls are stacked like bricks; towering walls extending to almost the height of the chamber. At the end of this line of dwarfs, in the center of these gold brick walls is a giant endless black cavern; a hole so deep that it seems to have no bottom. Sixteen dwarfs smash the clay bowls and drop the smelted gold ore down into the holes emptiness, again… again… and again.

In this large chamber is a large bone made structure, and from this structure is another line of dwarfs that follows the same path as the first line of dwarfs; all the way back to the gold spilling cauldron. These little people are passing empty clay bowls from the bone structure all the way to where the liquid gold is collected. Throughout this city are large posts with thousands of deer skulls fastened to the posts. Hanging from these deer skulls horns, are the corpses of animals large and small; in various stages of decay with their innards clumped in piles at the bottom of the poles.

Surrounding this city of bones… are a few hundred guards standing very still, watching the daily activities; they all wield a very menacing gold spear that looks like the mixture of a spear and a sword.

One of the guards starts to sniff… it starts to tilt his head back and sniff the air, the guard slowly turns his head to the right taking in deep breaths through its large oversized nostrils; and then its eyes lock with Fortier's bulging stare. The little man then stares curiously at Victor for a few moments, slightly tilting its head. The little man's infuriated eyebrows cast downward over half of its angry dark eyes, its tiny mouth drops open and a long terrifying screech sound fills the cave; it lifts its spear; pointing up at Fortier. The other guards start to look around for the one that is screeching, screeching a sound of alarm. As each guards eyes find the guard that is screeching, their eyes slowly follow the direction of where the little man is looking; as soon as they see Fortier they too start to screech; soon there is such a loud blood curdling screeching pitch vibrating off the cave walls. Fortier sees the guards now charging up a large bone staircase that hugs the cave wall on the other side of the cave. Fortier in absolute fear drops down from the boulder.

"RUN!" yelled Fortier as he quickly grabs the lantern leading his men as fast as he can up the sloped cave shaft.

In terror the men all run as fast as they can, they reach the top in seconds and now must climb over and through the mounds of bones. The men scamper and clamber up and down the mounds of bones, hearing the reverberating screeching getting closer. Down the last mound of bones the men run, Tetu trips and rolls down the mound; but he quickly recovers; breathing and gasping for air he begins to run again following the other men. Into the shaft entrance the men start to run, just before entering the shaft entrance Tetu decides to take a quick look backward and sees the silhouettes of the charging little people and the glint of their gold spears.

"OHHHHHHhhhhh CALISE TABRANAC FUCKING RUN! THEY ARE COMING!" yelled Tetu as loud as he could, now completely horrified; his eyes were so wide open they look like they could fall out.

Closer and closer the cave entrance light drew to them, brighter the cave walls started to light up. Their legs felt weak and were very heavy, each man feeling like they were separated from their legs. The two totems can now be seen, the men starting to lose their pace; their speed is starting to fail and with heavy stomping feet they clamber toward the entrance; now very close. Fortier and his men reach the totems and each man jumps and dives out of the cave with no energy left in them, hitting the hills hard surface. Fortier draws a knife from his belt trying to ready himself for a fight to the end.

"BASILE BRING A GUN, HURRY!" yelled Fortier as loud as he could as he was out of breath.

The men all turn their heads and stare at the cave entrance, hearing the screeching of the little people getting louder; they all stare with fear; waiting to meet their deaths. Basile racing up the hills slope and sees the men staring in fear at the caves black entrance. Basile immediately goes down to one knee and aims his rifle, ready for anything he stares into the black. The screeching now so loud it's piercing, then as the daylight strikes the dwarfs charging toward the entrance; everyone freezes in terror. Basile fires a shot into the cave entrance "POW."

The bullet hits one of the little men and it stumbles and falls, the other little people run over its body continuing their charge; the little men reach the entrance totems and completely stop; all they could do was screech and pace angrily by the totems.

"I don't think they can pass the totems, I think they are trapped by the totems." said Antin as he looked in disbelief.

"Look at them… they are absolutely hostile!" said Basile as he lowered his gun.

The screeching started to weaken and then it stopped. Staring from inside the cave the eyes started to disappear, the dark silhouettes slowly disappear into the cave; and then they were gone. The men all breathing with relief, their minds try to process what has just happened to them. Basile stands in front of the cave looking at the men, weak from the run of their lives; laying on the ground recuperating. After a short while the men slowly change to a sitting position in silence, Basile quietly stands with his arms crossed.

"PPffffffffeerrrrrrttttttt!" Basile farted… he turned to face the cave entrance.

"YOU ARE ALL GONEAIRS… I HAVE SINGLE HANDEDLY WIPED OUT YOUR CLAN OF MUNCHKINS… YOU ARE ALL ABOUT TO DIE A SLOW AND PAINFULL DEATH… BASILE WILL SHOW YOU… NO … MERCY… that one had extra gravy!" laughed Basile as he joined the other men who

were all already gut laughing, with Tetu again in tears; but this time it was of laughter. Basile always uses his humor to fix stressful situations, it eases his mind; and his friends… love him for it.

The men gathered their horses and continued to follow the large footprints until it was close to dark, hoping to travel as far away from that cave as possible. They setup camp for the night sitting around the camp fire they ate their supper, and told Basile and Tetu what they had seen in the bottom of that cave; exhausted and recovering from the terror; the men could not wait for a good night sleep. Fortier and the men all took turns on night watch, being as careful as they could; not to miss anything that could be lurking in the shadows.

The Climb   Day Seven

The men woke to a served morning breakfast, Basile made sure that there was enough to fill everyone for the morning's journey; they then broke camp and Fortier led the rescue party to find Marc.

"The tracks continue in this direction, it looks like they are headed for that dense bit of forest." explained Fortier.

"Keep your eyes open men… we don't want to end up walking into a trap." said Antin, and the men all casually scanned the forest for any signs; and any movement.

They near the dense part of the forest, the trees stand together; much too close for a horse to travel through. The tracks proceed into the forest, and the men must follow.

"Woooow… we need to continue on foot. Tie the horses and gather enough supplies for two days, we don't know how long we will be tracking in this part of the forest." said Fortier as he got off his horse.

"Do you think that's all we need for supplies?" asked Antin.

"Well what I am thinking is, if we can't find Marc within two days we will need to return to the horses to tend to them anyway; and we will need to find a way around this dense forest to continue our search." explained Fortier as he removed his rifle from his horse and placed the rifle strap over his head and hung it over his shoulder for carrying.

"I hope we find Marc soon… and I hope that creature hasn't hurt him." said Basile trying to be positive and holding onto hope.

Fortier and his men start their way into the dense forest, following the large foot prints left behind by an unknown creature. The men still hear no birds singing, no wind to be heard; almost no sound at all; only the crunching of the snow beneath their every step. The terrain seemed very flat with a small hill showing up once in a while. The trees were close together with no paths broken by animals, nothing to follow but the sun; this fact alone started to worry Fortier.

"Antin, I need you to start tying markers on the trees like Tarin did... I am starting to worry a bit because this forest is much too dense. There is no path or markers to follow and I am not sure if we would find our way back without them." explained Fortier as he looked around the forest knowing that he and his men could get lost very easily in there.

"I see exactly what you mean, I will get on that right now Fortier." ensured Antin as he tore two small pieces of material from his blanket and fastened his directional markers to two trees.

The men pressed on wondering when or if they were ever going to find Marc or Tarin or Andre, things seemed bleak for the men's success; but no one wanted to give up; the men all knew what they signed up for and they were going to see it through.

"Up ahead... there is a large hill, the trees seem to be taller and thicker there; it looks like that is where the tracks are headed!" stated Fortier giving the men a sense of hope.

The men arrived at the bottom of the large hill and examined the trees, they were much taller and much thicker than the trees they had been walking through.

"These trees are very different from anything we have been through or seen so far... these trees seem much older than the rest of the forest; I don't know... they just seem like they don't fit this environment?" said Fortier with confusion on his face as he touched and examined the very thick tree bark.

"Look at how tall they are... they are almost three times

taller than any tree we have seen, and they still have their green pines on them; it's the middle of winter!" explained Basile as he and all the men were puzzled by these strange trees.

"Well we better get moving… it's mid-day already." said Fortier as he looked at the suns position in the sky, eager to find Marc.

Sun rays streaked in through the forest trees causing shapely shadows on the forest floor, and twinkles of miniature bursts of light on the snow and ice covered ground. Snow sits on the thick branches adding beauty to the tiring uphill trek the men have to endure. Not a sound can be heard. Half way up the men stop for a short break.

"Ok, let's rest here for a while and have some dried meat." said Fortier to the men's approval.

The men cleared away some snow and sat on their blankets, so not to get wet when sitting. Resting up and eating for a bit of energy, the men sat and spoke quietly for a while.

"We are making pretty good time up this hill… It is not far off in comparison to the size of a mountain, this is a challenge for sure!" said Antin as he passed the bag of dried meat to Basile after tearing a piece of dried meat for himself.

"It is a pretty steep incline… we would have had to walk the horses up this anyway, it kind of helps that they are not here; other than us having to carry the supplies." said Tetu with a smirk on his face.

"Well… should we talk about it?" asked Fortier with a much more serious conversation in mind.

"Talk about what?" inquired Basile as he could see that Fortier really had something on his mind.

"Should we talk about what's going on?" asked Fortier with a bit of a sad look on his face, as he is starting to feel defeated.

"Yes… you are right, we probably should." answered Basile.

Fortier sitting… looking down at the snow he is piercing with a small twig he had found, Fortier looks up at his men and see's that he has their full attention.

"This rescue… this has turned into a task that would challenge the best of men, and push them to their very limits. The journey of these lands alone could break a man, but the things we have endured thus far; would break any man. The lands we have to conquer… the wild predators that hunt us… meeting new tribes of aboriginals is always a risk… and now it seems that we have crossed a threshold into a much different world. I have not seen or heard not one animal since we left the aboriginal families camp, only creatures of unknown origin; and the silence of the forests we encounter… it's very un-natural in a very menacing way. The only reasoning that can come close to the things we have witnessed so far is that these lands… are cursed!" said Fortier giving the men a feeling that he felt lost and overwhelmed by the strange events and forces upon them.

"There is definitely something wrong with these lands Victor… you're right, we need to find Marc, Tartin, and Andre and leave these lands as soon as we can; we don't belong here… like the aboriginals sacred grounds; we are not meant to cross them." said Antin with concern in his voice.

"That is probably why that warrior was trying to stop us… he sure didn't want us to enter the forest and follow in Tarin's tracks… he was definitely trying to warn us, and we didn't listen." reasoned Basile.

"We couldn't listen… and we still can't listen, his intentions were kind, meaningful and noble; but still we must find our missing men." said Fortier sympathetically to Basile's very wise account of what happened at the warriors camp.

"These are strange lands indeed... entering these lands must come with a cost... but at what cost... we need to find our missing friends and get out of here!" said Tetu in a desperate tone.

"This journey has already come with great cost... the loss of our friends... you're right Tetu, I just hope were not too late. Well, let's get up this hill and go find our friend." said Fortier as he got up off the ground and picked up his blanket.

The men all got up and started folding their blankets and started to follow Fortier up the mountainous hill. They kept a steady pace to conserve their energy, the climb was long and difficult; but they all finally reached the top.

"Let's setup camp here... it's late in the day, there won't be much sunlight left for us; we need to rest up; tomorrow is going to be a full day of searching." explained Fortier as the men were in full agreement, it had been a tiresome day.

With a small fire lit, the men sit tightly around the flames; eating their evening's dinner carrying on a quiet conversation.

"Victor... I noticed something and I have been meaning to bring it up... but with Marc missing, I didn't want to add to our problems. Have you noticed that ever since we left the warriors camp and entered the forest... Tarin and Andre..." said Antin, but was sharply cut off.

"Have not left any more markers on the trees...yes, I noticed that when we were looking for Marc's tracks at our last camp... that's why I wanted to concentrate on Marc's disappearance. I was hoping we would find Tarin's markers on our search for Marc... but now I am hoping that whatever has taken Marc... will also have Tarin and Andre... we can only hope." said Fortier reluctantly with despair in his eyes.

"Because there were no markers left by Tarin... I have come to the conclusion that not long after they left the warrior's camp,

someone or something has taken them. The only sign of them was their camp fire... where we too made camp not too far outside the warrior's meadow. That is where I think they disappeared." further explained Fortier trying to fill his men in on his thoughts of what may have happened.

"What the hell you guys... what are we going to do? How are we going to find them? What if they aren't with Marc?" questioned Tetu with worry trapped on his face.

"We have no markers to follow, and no tracks in the snow to track of Tarin and Andre. I am sorry... but if we find Marc, and Tarin and Andre are not with him... we cannot continue the search for them." said Fortier with a sad heart as he looked deep into the fire.

"If Marc had not gone missing and we had looked for Tarin's markers and found none, we would have had to end the search right there and then... we would have been on our way back to report to Jacques... I am sorry men." said Fortier having to bare the bad news.

"We will find Marc then... we have too." proclaimed Antin to the men, hoping that they would be up to the task.

"We need to get some rest... I will take first watch tonight. When it's your turn for night watch, stay here close to the fire. I am going to tie a rope around one of everyone's legs... no one is going to be taken tonight, I will wake you in four hours Tetu... sleep well everyone." ensured Fortier as he started to tie one of everyone's legs together, leaving slack for everyone to be comfortable.

All of the men fell fast asleep with Fortier watching carefully over them, he did not wake anyone for change of watch duty; he wanted to make sure no one went missing this night... he wanted this responsibility all on his own. Fortier stayed up all night, with no large creatures hidden in the shadows of the trees.

Protectors Of The Forest   Day Eight

Basile awoke… two hours before sunrise.

"Fortier… you're not supposed to be awake." claimed Basile quietly as he sat up.

"I took everyone's shift last night… I don't want anyone else to go missing, a responsibility I will hold alone." said Fortier quietly to Basile.

"I am going to make you a big breakfast… and then I want you to go to sleep for a few hours, I will wake everyone up for breakfast when you go to bed." said Basile as he started to gather eggs and dried meat from the supplies.

"What's on the menu this morning?" asked Fortier as he sat down where his blanket was.

"For you, I will make cooked dried meat, cindered in garlic and pepper accompanied by three… very… sunny side eggs soooo tasty the flutter-flies will want a tasty bite!" said Basile quietly with a smile.

"You did mean butterflies… didn't you?" asked Fortier with a quiet chuckle… trying not to laugh.

"Mon Dieu!… no… flutter-flies! They FLUTTER when they fly, they do not BUTTAIRE!" said Basile as he started to try and contain his laughter so not to wake the men.

Fortier was giggling and trying not to be loud.

"Will there be toast?" asked Fortier through his quiet laughter.

"We… French toast… but of course!" laughed Basile with Fortier… they both gut laugh as silent as they can, neither of them dare say another word in fear that the laughter would get out of hand.

After they had both settled down, Fortier and Basile both

enjoyed their breakfast together; as the black night sky was slowly starting to change to blue; just an hour before dawn. Basile enjoyed making his friends laugh, Basile really missed Demarr; and with every joke he told… he told it in Demarr's memory.

The men had all eaten quietly so not to wake Fortier as Basile had told them he was up all night. Basile waited two hours as agreed and then woke Fortier up.

"Fortier, the men are fed and ready… here is your coffee." said Basile as Fortier sat up.

They all sat together and had coffee looking down the hill at the top of the forest trees that they were going to venture into today, trying to enjoy the view but they knew something could be waiting for them… they all desperately wanted to find Marc.

The men start down the steep slope following the tracks left behind by the large forest creature. Further down they tread the steep and rocky hill side, and into the thick forest canopies shade they look for any clues. Fortier spots something odd and stops the men and crouched down.

"Do you see that?" whispered Fortier as he pointed to the right… not too far to the north.

Giant stacks of logs covered in moss and snow, they look clumsily piled up; but piled up none the less.

"Could that be some sort of make shift hut or dwelling?" whispered Fortier as he and his men stare off in the distance at the very well hidden structure, knowing that the tracks will probably lead there.

Down the slope the men walk… hoping that they will soon find Marc, hoping he is ok. The ground starts to level off and the tracks start to change direction… to the north. Nearing the area where they had seen the log structure… the men stop.

"*I want you men to stay here… I am going alone.*" said Fortier quietly to his men.

"*We are coming with you!*" explained Basile in a very upset and raspy whisper.

"*I have thought this out… last night while I was up all night, I didn't want to tell you guys because I knew you would demand to come. You can't come, if whatever has Marc; sees all of us; it will feel threatened… and could possibly kill one of us… or all of us. If it's going to kill any of us… it will be me. If you hear me screaming… you run back up this hill and down to the horses, follow the markers and get back to Jacques.*" whispered Fortier as he ordered his men.

"*Are you sure about this Victor?*" asked Antin with great concern on his face, saddened by what his friend was saying.

"*I have never been so sure about anything in my life Antin.*" reassured Fortier as he gave his bag of supplies to Antin and started to walk into the forest following the tracks… they could only watch as Fortier disappeared into the forest vegetation and trees.

Slowly Fortier walked listening to the pounding of his heart beat. Each step carefully placed so not to step on a branch or a twig, and then… he seen it. It was much more than a wooden structure… it was a village. Large tree trunks piled together making very primitive shelters scattered everywhere Fortier could see. No sign of fire or torches could be seen. Fortier then slowly walks into the village, careful with every move; every step. With his eyes squinting he tries to see inside one of the huts and finds a giant hairy creature sleeping. If he had to guess it would be nine feet tall. He could barely make out its face because of the hair, it looked more ape like than a man. It looked to have very large muscles all over its body, but its hair was so thick and long that no definition could be seen; the creature was absolutely terrifying to look at. They must be nocturnal thought Fortier. Fortier, as quiet as he could, he continued to slowly walk into the center of the village; looking into each hut as he passed by… searching for Marc. As Fortier neared the center of the village he starts to see a large hole dug in the ground, he slowly approaches the hole; slowly peering over its edge. Fortier's eyes finally find the bottom of the hole, and there laid Marc with dried up blood all over his face from a wound on his head. Fortier quietly stared at Marc hoping to see any movement, any sign of life; and then he saw his chest move with breath. Fortier slowly picked up a small rock and lightly tossed it at Marc's belly… but Marc did not wake. Fortier then picked up another small rock and tossed it at Marc and hit him on the head.

"Ahhh." said Marc as he slowly opened his eyes and rubbing his head.

As his vision clears he sees Fortier standing above with his finger over his lips, Marc's eyes slam wide open and he then presses his finger to his own lips. Fortier slowly starts taking off his coat and Marc slowly stands up. Fortier slowly lies down on the ground, careful not to make a sound; and lowers the coat into the hole while holding one of its arms. Marc clutches the coat arm as high as he could reach and jumps to grab the coats arm higher with his other hand. Pulling himself up with all of his might, he quickly frees one of his hands; and grabs Fortier by the arm. Fortier grabs Marc by the arm and starts to pull and roll over at the same time, sliding Marc's big body out of the hole that was dug as his prison. Fortier slowly puts his coat back on. Fortier turns and slowly steps back inside the footprints he had made to get to Marc, Marc follows Fortier's lead and does the same as he. Slowly and carefully… the two men re-trace Fortier's tracks back through the village. Neither Fortier or Marc look inside any of the huts, they are focused on not making a sound; they don't want to see the creatures anymore. They crept ever so quietly to make it to the edge of village, and continue to trace Fortier's tracks slowly as their hearts race inside their chests. Fortier and Marc make it back to the men, their faces light up with such happiness to see them both. They all walk quietly without saying a word back to the bottom of the hill, the men all take turns giving Marc a firm hand shake; and then Marc grabs Fortier and gives him a big hug.

The men start the long climb back up the hill, staying silent without a word. Basile reaches into his bag and pulls out a large piece of dried meat and gives it to Marc. Marc tore at the meat with his teeth and began to chew it as fast as his jaw could move. The men finally almost have reached the top of the hill; it is a slow and tiring trek.

They made it over the top of the hill and all the way down the hill to the forest tree line, where they spotted the markers Antin had put around the trees.

"Ok, let's hurry as fast as we can through these tight trees and get to our horses." ordered Fortier as quietly as he could.

Fortier and the men are now almost jogging through the trees, stumbling here and there over downed branches and rocks. They keep a steady pace so not to tire quickly. They reach the horses.

"RRRRRAAAAAAAAAAAAAAAAAAAAA!" the beast like roar filled the air from far off in the distance, from the other side of the mountainous hill.

"They must have woken up, it's about three hours before dark. Let's ride back out of here as fast as we can, and let's not stop for a few more hours into the night; far far from them!" said Fortier as he mounted his horse and kicked it into a gallop.

The men did the same and wanted to be far from those creatures. For hours they rode and did not tire, sunset had come and gone but they did not stop for supper. The snow was lit by the moon and they continued to ride for hours into the night, until Fortier had finally stopped his horse in the middle of the forest.

"Wooooow… let's make camp here, it's time to eat; we are starved Basile!" claimed Fortier as he climbed off his horse.

"I will make you all the finest din-aire composed like the finest sonnet your taste buds have eve-aire heard!" said Basile as he sifted through the supply bag.

"Wait… that… was the most confusing thing I have ever heard you say, what was that supposed to mean?" asked Antin with the same confused look as all the other men.

"WELL… I am SHOCKED! Absolutely AS-TON-ISHED! You mean to tell me you have never… EVER… NEVER EVER… had BAKED BROWN BEANS!" replied Basile trying not to smile, but the men were laughing to hard and he too joined them in laughter.

"A beautiful Sonnet… that we will all hear la-tair… it will be sung out of my rear!" laughed Basile as he shook the two jars of beans in the air.

The men all laughed and finally settled back down again. The fire was made and the men all sat around it and watched Basile make them all a fine celebration meal for Marc, coffee, eggs, toast, bacon, mushrooms, and yes… baked beans. As Basile was cooking, Marc told the men the story of what had happened to him.

"I was on my night watch and I went a little ways to have a piss, and then I heard something in the forest like a twig snapped; so I walked out a little further. The next thing I see in the flicker of light from the fire, something large and hairy not an arm's length

away. The next thing I know is my head is in a lot of pain, and I didn't dare make a noise; I was being carried by something much larger than me. All I could see was the back of it, I couldn't see anything but hair and the footprints it left behind in the moon lit snow; and I remember passing out from the pain again. The next time I became conscience, I woke in a hole that was dug too deep for me to climb out of. It was day time and I didn't hear anything, I stayed quiet... I didn't want them to know I was awake; I just played dead. I slept as often as I could... to try and sleep through the pain in my head. I woke up at night and I heard the strangest sounds... sounds that I have never heard from no animal or beast. I could hear them at the edge of the hole... they were communicating... like talking to each other, I kept my eyes closed; it was much too black for me to see but I knew they could see me. I could feel their eyes... I thought they were going to kill me, I stayed up all night with my eyes closed; pretending to be dead; I could hear giant CRACKS of busting tree trunks and roars of the angry creatures; it was the longest night I have ever had. When morning came everything was silent... there was no sounds at all, so I fell fast asleep. The next thing I remember was my head in pain, and I opened my eyes and I saw Fortier; I never wanted to yell and cry so badly; but I didn't... I knew if I did we would die." said Marc as he was handed his plate of food and started to eat.

"Well Marc... have we got a story to tell you." said Antin as he finished his plate of food, ready to tell the story of the little people in the cave.

The men finished telling their terrifying stories and got ready for bed, Fortier started tying the rope around Marc's leg.

"What are you doing?" asked Marc.

"I am not losing you again." said Fortier as he started tying it to Tetu next and then to Antin and so on.

"Fortier you are one very smart man." said Marc as he lay down with his blanket.

"I will take first watch here by the fire… after those stories there is no way I could go to sleep yet." said young Tetu.

Everyone went fast to sleep and Tetu sat by the fires warmth drinking coffee into the night.

Stick Man   Day Nine

The men woke to one of Basile's famous breakfast's, with no incidents in the night. The men un-tie themselves from each other and eat their hot meal, as the sun starts to break through the trees. The men ready the horses and pack up their supplies, and the discussion starts.

"Victor, so what is the plan for today?" asked Antin as he and all the men climbed onto their horses.

"Men, it is with a heavy heart that I say… the rescue mission is over, we have no way to track Tarin and Andre; so we are now going back east to report to Jacques Cartier. The terrain and the forest going back east there on the horizon, looks much too thick to travel through. We are going to head north today to look for easier terrain to travel… some open prairie would be wishful thinking, but a thinner forest would be great." said Fortier as the men could see he was upset that he had to abandon the search for Tarin and Andre.

"We are with you and your decision Victor… you really have no choice… we have nothing to go on to track them, your plan to go north sounds good." replied Antin trying to reassure Fortier he was making the only decision that he could make.

"We are almost through half of our food supplies, but we will have enough to make it back." said Basile ensuring the men that they would not starve, even with the northern detour.

"Alright then… north it is." said Fortier as he and the men kicked their horses in line and started north.

For hours they traveled north hoping for the east forest to thin out so they could travel through, but they had seen no change in the density of the trees. The hours that pass seem so much longer, no birds to watch or listen to; no animals scurrying about the forest floor; not a sound; and it affects the men senses everyday making every hour of everyday seem longer.

"There… it looks like an old path, let's have a look." said Fortier as he and the men approached the break in the trees.

A worn old trail that seemed to weave through the forest, just wide enough for their horses to pass through.

"It looks like a very old trail… might have been made by the aboriginals long long ago, it doesn't look like an active trail; I think it might be safe to try." said Antin as he tried to reason the trails use.

"We really don't have much choice now, this looks like our best chance… let's see if it will take us to the other side of the forest… be sure your rifles are loaded." said Fortier and the men checked their rifles as ordered.

On to the trail the men directed their horses, slow curvy turns through the tree stalks; the trail twisted in the forest; up and down hills that made the forest floor. Thousands of trees in every direction, that seemed like infinity; tree's that look like one solid mass as they drive their horses deeper into the forest. The tree's feel haunting even in the suns light, barren of leaves the tree's sickly twisted limbs and branches seem to band together; preventing anyone or anything from straying from the trail they were on.

"Alright let's have lunch!" yelled Fortier and everyone stopped their horse.

"Now that's a great idea… I am starved." replied Marc as he got down from his horse.

All of the men worked together to gather wood and helped retrieve the items of food requested by Basile from the supply bags, and soon they were all eating and warming by the fire.

"I feel like I am going crazy... it's this forest... its emptiness... like we are the only ones alive in it." said Tetu abruptly with no warning and a sad look on his face.

With a look of concern Fortier quickly grabs Tetu's shoulder and grasps it firmly.

"Tetu... you are not the only one that feels this way, I think we all are feeling the effects of this entire forest... you are not alone. I try to think of my children back in France, at home helping their mother with the daily chores. I know you are a young man and have no children, but what I am saying is you need to think of other things; good things to take your mind away from here. Distract your mind with fun and good thoughts... it will help you... it will get you through." said Fortier with helpful advice.

"That works for you?... I will try it, thank you Fortier; and I am sorry for ruining lunch; it was just starting to really drive me mad." explained Tetu.

"It is imposs-i-ble to ruin this mag-nif-i-cent and most impressive lunch we are having... French toast, dried fish cooked in butter and garlic, and but of course... magnifique... pep-aired eggs! You could not ruin this lunch even if you had EXPLOSIVE diarrhea and shit in your trous-aires, giving yourself a shit-back and sprays us all in the face... no; it is impossible to ruin this refined din-aire!" laughed Basile as all the men too were laughing at his ridiculous speech.

"There... you feel better?" asked Basile of Tetu as the laughter calmed down.

"Yes, much better." said Tetu as his laughter started to calm down.

"Well I don't know about any of you... but I need to take a dump before I get... SHIT-BACK!" said Marc as he laughed and

walked into the forest.

The men all settled down and cleaned up their lunch dishes and started to put them away.

"HEY... where is Marc?" asked Basile quickly.

Everyone had a puzzled look on their faces which quickly turned to panic.

"MARC!" yelled Fortier as he and the men started to run into the forest in the same place Marc had entered, but there was no answer.

Fortier and the men all followed Marc's tracks into the forest and then they see Marc, lying in a pool of blood with a wooden pike spear stuck through his neck.

"MARC! Sacre bleu! What in God's name has happened?" questioned Fortier as he and his men look down onto Marc's lifeless body. Beside his body a large gold coin could be seen on the ground.

"Uhhhhh... what is that?" asked Antin as he looked into the forest not far from where they stood.

The all stared at a very strange artifact... a very strange wooden object, carved and made to look like a very small man; a wooden man that was only three feet tall. Motionless stood this oddity in the middle of nowhere, in the middle of this forest.

"What is this?" questioned Fortier as he walked to the wooden stick man.

Fortier cautiously approached the figure, studying its features as they became clearer as he got closer; and then he notices another large gold coin at the stick man's feet. Fortier slowly bends down and reaches his hand out to pick up the gold coin and then stops himself, he then says to himself in a quiet whisper,

"Don't take it." whispered Fortier as he froze himself of all movement.

"Look at the size of this gold coin and why did Marc have it?" asked Tetu as he held the coin.

"NOOOOOOO, Drop it Tetu!" yelled Fortier as he turned his head to look at Tetu.

A wooden pike spear flew just past Fortier's head from behind him, from where the stick man stood. The wooden pike slammed into Tetu's chest. Tetu fell to his knee's as his mouth falls open, his body hit's the ground beside Marc's.

"OH MY GOD! TETU!" yelled Basile as he dove to catch Tetu as he fell to the ground. Fortier runs to Tetu, he and the men surround Tetu and try to comfort him.

"I'm sorry..." said Tetu with his last breath as his eyes then rolled back beneath his eye lids.

"Nooo, Tetu... Nooo!" cried Fortier as he looked at the wooden pike sticking out of Tetu's chest.

"What is that thing! Why did it kill them?" questioned Basile as he wiped tears from his eyes.

"The gold... I don't think anyone is supposed to take it from the Stick Man." guessed Fortier as they stared at the Stick Man.

"It must be cursed, or some kind of heretic magic, or an evil spirit... I don't know, but it's evil... it's a trap!" questioned and reasoned Fortier as he tried to understand the phenomenon that stood lifeless and motionless in front of them.

Fortier, Antin, and Basile all gathered wood to build proper burial tombs for Marc and Tetu. After long, the tombs were built and a quiet prayer was said for the men. The three men mount their horses, and each of them are now towing the extra horses that carry the supplies.

"We should set that wooden Stick Man on FIRE!" said Antin as he turned and looked back at it.

"I was thinking the same thing… but what if that cursed thing comes to life again because we set it on fire… then we will all die… we have no choice but to leave it as it stands in these cursed lands." explained Fortier who so wanted to set it on fire as much as Antin did.

With a short kick to the side of their horses, the men started back down the trail in the forest. The men started to see something familiar up a head in the forest.

"Fortier isn't that… over there… a Stick Man holding a wooden pike?" asked Basile as he pointed at what he saw.

"Over there… there is another one!" said Antin as he pointed in another direction.

"Another… there!" said Antin.

"There are a bunch of them over there!" said Basile with his face starting to show fear.

"Keep quiet now… let's just keep our courage about us and get through this forest." said Fortier quietly to the men.

As the men continued into the forest, more and more of the Stick Men began to appear; large groups of them each standing in front of a large gold coin. On ward they drove their horses down the trail, past the few hundred Stick Men scattered in the forest trees. Fortier thought to himself that he was glad that he and his men had not set that Stick Man on fire, he couldn't help but think that he and his men would have died by the pike spears of all the other Stick Men in the forest; almost knowing that they would have almost certainly come to life and came for him and his men. All Fortier and his men could do was look into the forest and hope that none of the Stick Men would come after them.

Very deep into the forest now, the men start to notice that the Stick Men started to thin out in their numbers; and then finally there were no more of them to be seen. It was nearing sun set now and the men's hunger was getting bothersome.

"Fortier, I know we are all hungry but I don't want to stop yet; unless you really want to." said Baslie as he was afraid the Stick Men would somehow appear in the forest.

"Your fear is felt by us all... it doesn't look like this forest is going to end in the next few hours, we are going to end up setting up camp in here. So, we will ride until near dark; as far away from those wooden curses as we can and then set up camp." said Fortier not wanting to stop at all, because he knew not stopping all night would not get them out of this enormous forest.

The sun was soon to set, Fortier stopped his men and they all set up camp; and Basile cooked dinner with no jokes to be heard. They all looked in the forest and no Stick Men could be found.

"This trail is so long... this forest is so large it seems to never end." said Antin as he was feeling like he was losing all hope.

"It really feels that way... but it is just our minds working against us, just remember to try and fill your thoughts with happier times... it is all any of us can do to ignore our own negative thoughts." said Fortier as he tried to give some advice, advise he himself needed to hear.

The men got ready for bed. Fortier tied one leg from each man to each other. Basile offered to take the nights first night watch, he had made a fresh pot of coffee and sat in his sleeping spot by the fire. Watching over the men he sipped on his coffee and watched the flicker of light in the forest from the night's camp fire. Basile thought he might have seen something strange far off in the forest, like the flail of a piece of cloth or clothing. He stared and stared but didn't see anything more; he changed his attention back to the nights fire feeling it was just the fire's light playing tricks on him. He stared into the fire, his mind sunk into the trance of the dancing of the flames; lost in the fire; lost in his stare. Basile's eyes felt very tired and very heavy, and with each moment his eye's slowly started to close; lost in the gaze of the fire. Basile did not notice how heavy his eyes were, how tired and sleepy he now was; his eyes were now almost completely closed; nothing he could do; he wanted to do nothing. Basile could not fight his eyes from shutting, did not want to fight it; and then his eyes were shut.

Asleep... am I asleep... almost asleep... sleep...... whose voice was that?

RICHARD HERRON

Is This How We Die   Night Nine

It starts as a quiet annoyance… can barely be heard or understood.

"UhhhbhshabauxgyeELP uhhhhhhhhbwgdgxEEE."

Again…but still un clear.

"UhhhkjncjuenenhELP uhhhhhhhwbwbyxbmEEE."

The mind is starting to clear… but all is still dark.

"UhhhhhsbdbeyeHELP uhhhhhhhbjawbjwMEEE."

Now the sound is clear… still dark… I can't open my eyes.

"UHHHH… HELP…. UHHHHHH… MEEE!"

My eyes open like a shutter… but only for a quick moment. That fraction of time… a large fire… the silouette of… so dark.

"HELP MEEE…. HELP MEEE… HELP MEEE!"

Trying to force my eyes to open… seems impossible… I yell as I struggle to pry my eye lids to open, why won't they open; why aren't they open. Weak… I feel very weak. Like coming out of the deepest sleep, something that could only be described as magic or a curse; my body finally awakens.

"UHHHHHHHHHHHHhhhhhhh WHAT THE FUCK, WHAT THE FUCK!"

I screamed as the sense of feeling returned to my body. My arms were in agonizing pain, as were also the front of my legs and chest. I feel that I am in a sitting position with my legs stretched out in front of me… my arms have been secured behind me against something very hard and rough. My eyes are blurred from the blood in my eyes, I blink and shake my head to try and clear my vision; still screaming in so much pain. Why am I in pain, I cannot see; my eyes are burning and irritated. I can finally see… I can see why I am in pain, why I am screaming; this is horrific… this is a nightmare. My legs and chest have been torn open, the flesh ripped and scratched in many strips; the skin flails open hanging by threads of my tissues. Hours must have past… the blood is dark and no longer flowing, no longer exiting from my wounds. A large fire blazes in front of me… crying I look into its flame. I look to my left and I see Antin tied to a large wooden stake that is buried deep into the ground, sitting slumped over with his hands tied behind his back around the large steak; one of his legs is missing; taken from the knee. I look to my right as I am still trying to clear the blood from my eyes, I see Fortier in the very same position as Antin and I. Fortier's chest has many lacerations, many over lapping cuts; that can only be described as claw marks from an animal; still unconscious. I then see him… the voice I have been hearing… the voice that is screaming… its Tarin. Tarin is screaming and his eye lids have been removed, he stares and screams at a body secured to a stake beside him; a body that has been stripped of its skin; only a torso… arms… and head remained; it was Andre. Something in the dark catches my eyes… behind Tarin… a ways behind Tarin, the fires light catches two hollow eyes glinting in the flames flicker. Without a sound and without movement, it could have been an animal… but a human nose can now be seen in the flickers of light; but nothing else. I have frozen in fear… I can feel shock starting to set in as my heart races. The two eyes just stare… the eyes, they listen to Tarin's screams and pleas for help; they just stare. Then, after moments of time has past; the eyes can barely be seen getting closer… very… very slowly getting closer; not changing position but they only twitch slightly; they don't seem to blink; these very large black eyes that shine two hollow white dots in the flicker of the fire. Closer and closer the eyes seem to float or creep toward the screaming and crying Tarin, no emotion; no change in position; these two eyes slowly approach... Tarin. Without warning, without a movement of the eyes; what seems to be a large tree branch swings in from out of the darkness; striking Tarin in the head and knocking him out... knocking him silent. I can feel my eyes bulging from my eye lids as I stare at the eyes, my pain is pushed out by the terror and fear; as I watch the eyes slowly backing away and then stop. The eyes now lock onto my eyes.

"They see me." whispered Basile to himself as he has been quiet, silenced by the fear of what is taking place; silenced by those eyes.

The eyes now slowly start to circle toward his right... very... very slowly, away from Tarin and toward Basile; the eyes slowly approach Basile from the shadows; just out of reach of the fires light flicker. Closer and closer move these hollowed out specs of light, these eyes near Basile; Basile hears a haunting exhale of breath; a sharp pain on his head and then everything goes black.

Circle Of Friends   Day Ten

The sun rises slowly in the sky. A smaller fire burns with its smoke bellowing into the sky, capturing the morning sun's rays as the smoke thins and disappears. A small and very makeshift wooden house sits not far from the fire, covered in moss and dead vines were the house's planks; with planks so old and rotten; the house looks like it could collapse at any time. Five posts surround the fire, evenly spaced around its flames; some start to wake in this circle of friends; some will wish they were already dead.

"Calise! Oh my God!" said Fortier as he started to tremble from the pain of his wounds on his chest and legs.

Fortier looking around franticly seeing his friends tied to the posts, trying to be silent; knowing he is still in danger. Looking around for any sign of his captor, but no captor can be seen. Fortier struggles to try and free his tied hands, but he can feel they are tied tight; and tied very well. Fortier now looking at his men and notices Tarin with his eye lids cut off and the gashes on his chest and legs… and then notices what is left of Andre… tears start to fall down his cheek. Basile starts to wake.

"Quiet… Quiet Basile, try not to make any noise; don't scream… please don't scream!" said Fortier pleading with the barely conscience Basile.

"Uhhhhhhhh… I saw something last night." replied Basile as his body started to shake from the pain, and stopping himself from wailing in agony.

"What was it that you saw Basile?" asked Fortier, but Fortier almost didn't want to know; afraid to know; afraid of what could have them here; could be anything unimaginable from inside this cursed forest.

"I … I saw eyes… like the glowing hollowed out eyes of an

animal when the light of a fire enters them... but I also seen a human nose... so I know this is no animal... I'm scared Victor. " whispered Basile as he started to quietly cry.

"So am I... " replied Fortier trying to hold back his tears.

Fortier looking around at anything and everything, he notices many... many Stick Men scattered inside the forest tree's around this hidden acreage.

"We must be somewhere in the same forest, there are Stick Men all around us just inside the tree line. " said Fortier to Basile who was cringing from the pain.

"Ahhhhhh... what, why do I feel... FUCK!" said Antin as he awoke in agony.

"Quiet Antin, hold in your screams... don't scream!" begged Fortier as quietly as he could.

"Ok... ok... what... is... happening? Why am I all cut up?" asked Antin silencing his screams and quivering in shock.

"We don't know... we are trying to figure this out. " replied Fortier with helplessness on his face.

"We don't want to make noise, so not to wake whoever is in that house. " said Basile pleading with Antin to be silent.

The sun slowly rises and its rays start to break over the trees, slowly removing the men from the shadows of the forest trees; rays of light striking the men in the face.

"AHHHHHHHH AHHHHHHHHHH AHHHH AHHHHHHHH AHHHHHHHHHHHHHHHH AHHHHHHHHH!" Screamed Tarin as the sun light struck his eyes and he woke in tortured pain.

"Stop Tarin Stop!" pleaded Fortier quietly as Tarin screamed and whipped his head from side to side violently, un able to close his eyes.

"Stop... please stop. " begged Fortier quietly as Tarin continued to scream and scream... and scream.

"Pretend to sleep!" whispered Basile to Fortier as he slumped his head; Fortier did the same; not to make a sound.

"SOM-AI-TATUM… KA-SAAA-RA… KA!… NE!" came the words from inside the house, yelled by what sounded like an old woman; scratchy and cracked was this voice they heard.

The door could be heard as it flung open, and banged against the house; muffled by the continuous screams of Tarin. Fortier and Basile keep their eyes shut… careful not to move, careful not to look; and hiding the pain they are suffering.

From the door… slowly… very slowly, silently she creeps; almost floating toward Tarin; who is uncontrollably screaming and lashing in such pain. Her eyes are locked on him through her depleting thin, white and black, straggly hair. She wears a worn and aged black shawl and black dress, holes and tears riddle her garments. She creeps steadily closer… and closer to the wailing Tarin, staring with her overly large black eyes. She stops right beside him staring at him as he screams and flails, slowly and almost without any movement; she slowly starts to crouch down… not moving her head; almost floating down ward with her worn dress starting to crumple as more gathers on the ground. Her very slow movement stops, her eyes now level with Tarin's face; as he continues to scream and flail with no control. Basile, unable to fight his growing urge to look, to see what is happening; slowly he starts to peek from one of his eyes; he barely wedged it open. Basile sees their captor… A witch, an old and almost ancient woman; staring at Tarin… inches from his screaming and thrashing face. Quickly, with one violently swift motion… an old curved blade of a rusting knife; slashes Tarin's throat… spilling blood onto his chest; spraying the witches face… and then it stops. The gargling screams stop, the blood slowly stops pumping out of Tarin's neck; Tarin stops moving and slowly slumps over. The witch slowly reaches down to Tarin's leg and digs her claw like nails into his legs flesh, she slowly tears a chunk of his flesh and places it in her mouth; she slowly begins to chew and savor its bloody flavor. Basile's eyes start to rain from sadness and fear, he forgets to keep his eyes shut as they are now wide open; and in his silent weeping; a small noise is made from his shuddering inhale of breath; a tiny sound. The witch's eyes whip to look at Basile, without moving her head. She stares into Basile's very open eyes, like a stone sculpture; he is frozen in terror. The witches head slowly… very slowly, starts to turn with her one eye concentrated on Basile's eyes; slowly her other eye comes into view; as it now too is staring into Basil's eyes. Slowly her head continues to turn, until her face is aligned directly at Basile; her head finally stops; she stares for moments; she stares. Basile now starts to uncontrollably whimper as he tries to hold in his cries and screams. She stares… she stares, her hidden arm slowly starts to rise up, and the blood splattered blade now starts to immerge from her billowed clothing. Slowly it rises up… slowly, and then it stops; and she stares. Without warning, she quickly hobbles from side to side; in a crouched walk; strait at Basile; as her mouth opens she lets out the loudest shrieking scream; that hits Basile with pain in his ears.

"EEeeeeerrrrrrrrrraaaaAAAAAAAAAAAAAA!" shrieked the witch moving full force at Basile. Fortier dared not to open his eyes, not for one moment; not even a flinch as his ears were in pain. Basile yelled as quickly as he could, to warn Fortier before his imminent death.

"SHE'S A WITCH!" screamed Basile as his final words of warning.

The knife blade sunk quickly into his chest, piercing Basile's heart… he quickly slumps over; Basile… is dead. Fortier does not move… dares not make a sound, he tries now to think of his wife

and children with his eyes closed. This may be his last moments alive… he wants them to be in his last thoughts… thoughts of his family, he sees his young daughter and son playing in the field of crops; running through the wheat. His wife in the suns gaze, hanging the family's clothes outside on a clothes line to dry. Filling his thoughts with these images, Fortier is completely silent; and ready to die in the blackness of his mind. Fortier hears the sounds of logs hitting the fire, with a crack and pop; the fire slowly gets bigger; igniting the newly placed logs.

"Screeeeech SLAM!" the door slammed shut on the little house and then nothing but silence was heard by Fortier.

Fortier holds his eyes shut, not to open them; afraid this could be a trick… did she go in or was she still outside? Fortier keeps his eyes closed, pretending to sleep; pretending to be dead; for hours… and hours… and hours. It has been many hours since the sun had left Fortier's face, no longer smudging the darkness of his eyelids; with muted light. It must be night, Fortier can feel warmth and is thankful for the heat of the fire; he does not wish to look and see all of his dead friends. He wants to move… he wants to break the ropes that bind his hands together, but he can't move, not until he knows it's safe to move; safe to struggle to get the rope off his wrists; Fortier must open his eyes to see if it is safe to struggle… to break free. With Fortier's head slumped to the side, his hands tied to a wooden pike behind his back; and his legs strait out in front of him; in agonizing pain… Fortier decides to open his eyes. Fortier counts down inside his mind… un… due… twa…

"WHOLY FUCK, OH MY GOD, NOOOOOOOOOOOOO!" screamed Fortier.

Fortier had opened his eyes and seen the witches face just inches from his, her head cocked looking up at him because he was slouched over; with her black eyes now locked onto his; her scowling face just stared at him through his panic and screams; the fires light flickered the shadows on her face. Had she been there all day… all those hours… just staring at Fortier as he pretended to be dead, for hours… and hours… yes she did.

"NOOOOOOOOOOOO PLEASE NOOOOOOOOOO!" Fortier continued to yell and scream, pleading for his life.

Staring at him as he uncontrollably screamed, the witch slowly started to raise her arm; with her head still cocked and twisted looking up at Fortier. A knife blade slowly begun to rise, and started to appear in Fortier's sight; Fortier's screams got louder and filled with panic. This was the end, there was nothing Fortier could do but look in terror; the witches knife slowly stopped; she stares at him for moments… only moments… and then,

"Pffffffffffttt!" a strange sound… and then an arrow pierces the witches head and she drops dead on the ground, slightly jumping and twitching; as her body is figuring out that it is dying and starts to shut down. Fortier staring at the dying witch stops screaming and starts gasping for air, he starts frantically looking into the black of night to see where the arrow came from; and then Great Eagle emerges from the darkness of the night. Fortier starts to uncontrollably cry and wail, weak and helpless he cries and can't believe he is going to live. Great Eagle bends down and cuts the ropes that bind Fortier's hands; Fortier falls to the ground crying in absolute pain and shock. Great Eagle picks up a heavy tree branch and hits Fortier on the head knocking him out.

"Sleep brother… sleep." said Great Eagle, and he grabbed a blanket from his horse and covered Fortier up for the night.

In Silent Prayer   Day Eleven

Morning had come. The sun was now just above the tree canopy, warming all that was below. Fortier started to open his eyes and sat up. He looked at the fire that was barely still lit, but in it was the witches burning old bones. He looked around and saw that his friends had been cut away from the posts and they were gone. Fortier started looking around and seen Great Eagle just finishing a nicely fashioned tomb, made of wood for all of his friends that lay side by side at peace in it. Fortier struggled and got to his feet, his legs burning in pain from the many wounds exposed through his torn pants. Grunting in pain, Fortier walked over to Great Eagle and placed his hand on his shoulder.

"Thank you." said Fortier in a soft voice.

Fortier stood in silent prayer for he did not have the words to express, how dearly his friends would all be missed; he stood silent for a while as his tears fell off his cheeks.

Fortier thought of Antin and how dedicated, loyal, and kind he was; a wonderful friend… best of friends. Tetu was a young man, learning all that he could as an explorer; and was given so little time here on earth; but made it very clear that he had a good heart; and shared his friendship with those who deserved it. Marc was a strong and silent man, he liked to help others… no matter how difficult the task; a kind and gentle giant. Demarr was like a big brother to Basile, he was very witty and enjoyed laughter; he never left Basile's side… like a shadow to his best friend; loyal until the end. Basile loved to cook for his friends, he loved that he was providing them with life for another day; by feeding them food and filling them with laughter; a man who will truly be missed by all those lucky enough to know him. The sadness Fortier was feeling was nearly unbearable, these thoughts of his friends in silent prayer; captured only the very essence of these men… but they were much much more; they were family… they were his brothers.

"We must go. " said Great Eagle as he pointed to the horses of Fortier's friends… and his.

"You found our horses? " replied Fortier who was surprised and relieved.

Great Eagle did not respond but he understood what Fortier had meant. Great Eagle bandaged up Fortier the best he could with the medical supplies from one of the bags. He helped Fortier onto his horse and handed him a string of horses to tow; Great Eagle too took a string a horses to tow. Great Eagle struck his horse and lead the way for Fortier to follow. The two men rode in silence, as silent as the forest they were in. The trees themselves move outward to widen the path for Great Eagle, as he and Fortier slowly make their way through the trail; Fortier was astonished by this mystical site; like the forest was making way for this honourable warrior.

Soon Fortier sees an unfamiliar site in this forest. A red fox sitting at the trails edge, staring and watching Great Eagle as he passes; after they pass… the little red fox jumps up and runs into the forest seemingly happy. Great Eagle had rid the forest of the witch, and now the forest animals can return. Further down the trail Fortier can see wolves… and bears… and deer… and moose… and birds, all waiting along the sides of the trail; as to say… thank you. After Great Eagle and Fortier pass the animals, the animals all make their way into the forest; in various directions; each to claim their own territory.

About late afternoon… they were making their way through the trees and snow covered ground, Fortier then sees a familiar site; two trees covered in skulls and bones; surrounded by green trees that were full of life. Fortier started to smile as they entered the enchanted meadow where Great Eagle and his family lived. Many birds could be heard singing and playing throughout the meadow. Great Eagle helped Fortier off of his horse and sat him next to the fire. Star and Little Fire came out from inside the tee-pee. Little Fire waved at Fortier and had run off in the meadow to play, Star started to cook some fish for everyone; and Great Eagle went to the horses and grabbed all the supplies bags and put them near Fortier. Fortier fumbled in the bags and brought out some items to cook. They all sat and ate, sharing the food together smiling; happy knowing what it truly means to live… to be thankful for every moment of everyday… thankful to those who are good and kind.

The sun starts to set and Star had just finished bandaging up Fortier's wounds with forest medicine. Fortier, exhausted and weak; lies beside the fire and covers himself with his blanket; and slowly closes his eyes. Great Eagle, Star, and Little Fire all look at each other and they too go to bed; and they disappear into the tee-pee for the night.

Ju Ju Man   Night Eleven

The night is dark. No moon in the night sky. Only the stars shine in the abyss above. Not a sound could be heard, all except the light crackle of the night's fire. It starts… as a light low rumble, the earth slowly starts to vibrate; greater and greater the rumbling earth starts to shake. It intensifies shaking the ground that all call their bed. Fortier awakes as the ground shakes violently; confused he looks around aimlessly in all directions. Only Great Eagle emerges from the tee-pee and walks to Fortier, as they both stand as they try to balance as the ground shakes.

"CRACK CRACK CRRRRRRRRAAAAAAACCCKKKK!" the sound of many trees busting and falling in the forest, far off in the distance; but the sound was moving closer… and closer. Fortier and Great Eagle could hear the destruction coming toward them from the spirit worlds forest, now sounding like a hundred rolls of thunder; shaking their ear drums as it approached; getting far too close now just outside the meadow. The sound suddenly stops, the earth stops shaking; and all the green vibrant trees started to shake around the meadow; leaving Fortier and Great Eagle standing clueless as to what is happening.

"Great Spirit… who are you?" asked Great Eagle.

"JUUUUuuuuuuu JUUUUuuuuuu Maaaaaannn." answered the Great Spirit, as the trees and its branches formed a large face; a form it chose to take; a form the men would recognize.

"What wakes you Great Spirit?" quickly asked Great Eagle.

"Strange man cannot leave this meadow… he has seen the spirit world… he must not leave!" answered the Great Spirit as the trees shook violently from its voice.

"How do I make him stay?" asked Great Eagle.

"Must not leave… OR HE MUST DIE!" roared the Great

Spirit shaking the meadow.

Great Eagle looks at Fortier and tries to explain.

"You can't leave here… you must stay!" said Great Eagle as he pointed at Fortier and then pointed at the ground. Great Eagle pointed to the east… and then slowly waved his hand in a swipe motion; and pointed once again at the gound.

"I'm not sure… you want me here? To stay here? I can't stay… I must go back!" said Fortier un-sure if he understood what Great Eagle was trying to tell him.

"TELL HIM!" roared the Great Spirit.

Great Eagle then took a moment to think. Great Eagle then walked up to Fortier and stood beside him and pointed yet again east, and then quickly put a knife blade to his throat. Fortier's eyes widened, careful not to move. Great Eagle then lowered the knife from Fortier's throat, pointed at Fortier with the knife… and then pointed at the ground.

"OK, I think I understand… I can't go back… or I will die." said Fortier as he then pointed at himself and then pointed at the ground; he nodded his head yes in agreement.

"He stays… he stays!" said Great Eagle to the Great Spirit.

"HE STAYS!" roared the Great Spirits voice as the forest trees shook once more, and then… the great spirit vanished.

Fortier sat by the fire staring into its flicker, Great Eagle had gone to bed with his family. Lost in the fire… Fortier's thoughts wandered. He thought of how he could never go back home, never see his family again; and never tell the tale of his journey…

A journey untold…

RICHARD HERRON

A Note From The Author

This story was written of a time when the First Nations Aboriginals of Canada and the settlement colonies were friendly to one another, a time… that has been forgotten; it is a sad truth of Canada that at one time everyone got along and now we live in a so called civilized age and time… where there is mostly racism toward Aboriginals.

It is 2020... Society is supposed to be more… civilized, I have heard from community members and seen video footage of the horrible treatment of Canadian Aboriginals; and it needs to stop. Aboriginal hockey teams being cursed at, spit at, and racial slurs hurled at them; by small town white Canadians when they play hockey in these small towns; and these Aboriginal teams players are 18-19 years old; but it has also happens to the small children that are aged 8-15 years old. The scars these children must suffer… the ridicule and hate that they must endure just to play a game that they as children… just want to enjoy and participate in. The white parents shouting at these children… these babies… is atrocious, evil and cruel; just think an entire community of parents treating these children in such a vulgar way; I can't find a word that completely or properly captures the amount of disgust I have for these parents… there is no word that covers the cowardice these parents portray. Then you have referees that are calling the game one sided, handing out penalties to the Aboriginals, and turning a blind eye to the white Canadian team… and yes this happens… and I have seen this happen… and this is only community hockey games; never mind the Aboriginals everyday normal interactions in stores or just walking in public.

Canadian society is so concerned these days about how we Canadians treat issues of immigration, immigrants, gender appropriation, Muslim issues, government scandals, gays, homo phobia, etc… and the list goes on in the forefront of issues that are actually being dealt with; but there is an issue that has not been dealt with and has been un-resolved for over 500 years and Canadians just turn a blind eye to the Aboriginal issue… letting the racism continue to sink its claws into society; letting the Aboriginal racism be swept under the rug and not cared about.

So why, as a Canadian fiction book writer… why am I writing this note in my book… because someone needs to go on record and say… racism against Canadian Aboriginals fills Canada from coast to coast… it needs to be addressed… and it needs to end.

Copyright Notice

Copyright

The author and publisher have provided this book to you for personal use only. You may not make this book publicly available in any way. Copyright infringement is against the law. If you believe the copy of this book you are reading infringes on the authors copyright, please notify the publisher.

Copyright

This is a work of fiction. All of the characters, organizations, and events portrayed in this novel are either products of the author's imagination or are used fictitiously and commissioned for Vicki Herron. All photos and art work by Richard Herron taken in and in surrounding areas of Frog Lake First Nation.

First Book Edition: January 12, 2020

ISBN 978-1-387-94781-2

All editing and structure formatting was conducted by Richard Herron. All rights reserved.

RICHARD HERRON

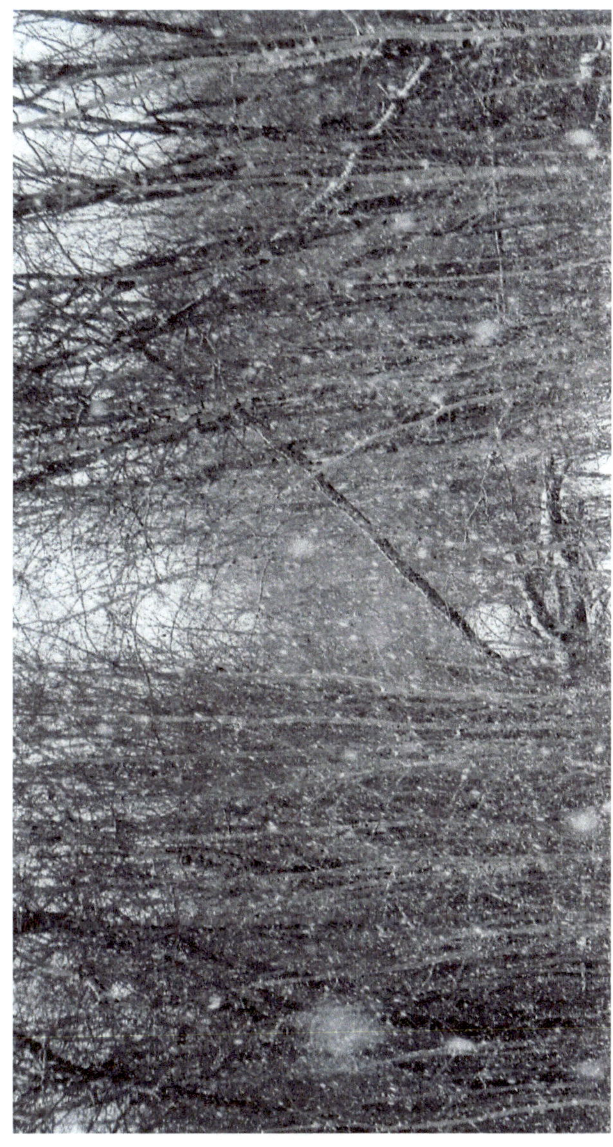

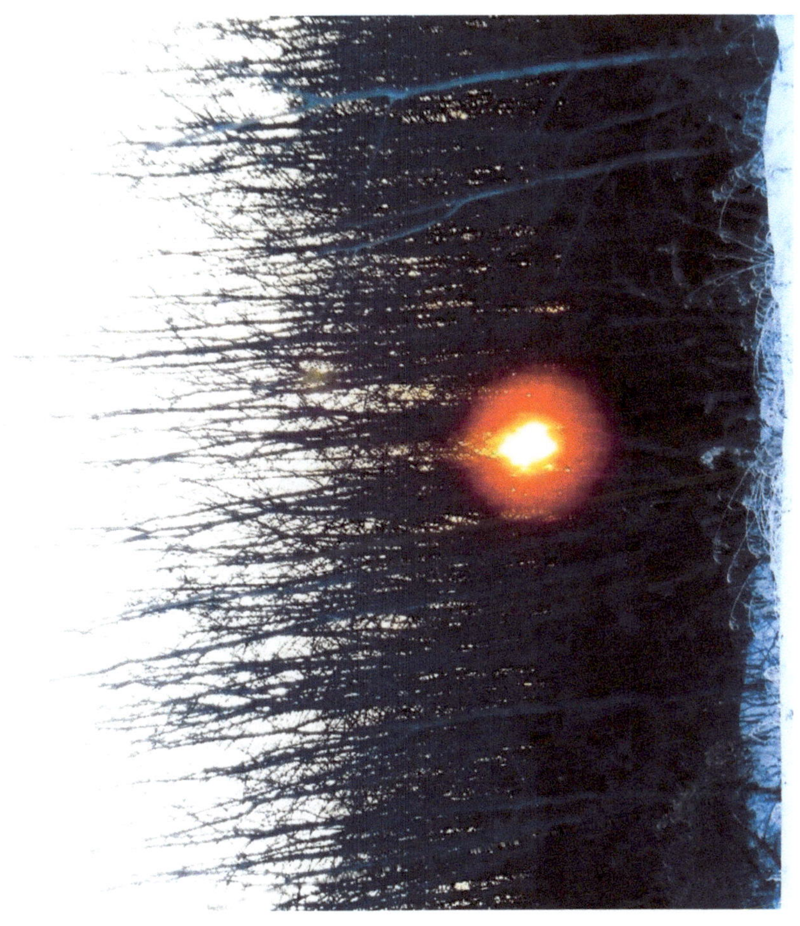

RICHARD HERRON

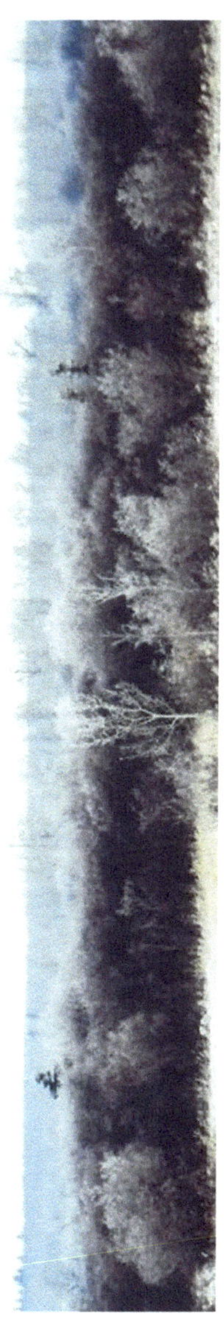

RICHARD HERRON

RICHARD HERRON

RICHARD HERRON

RICHARD HERRON

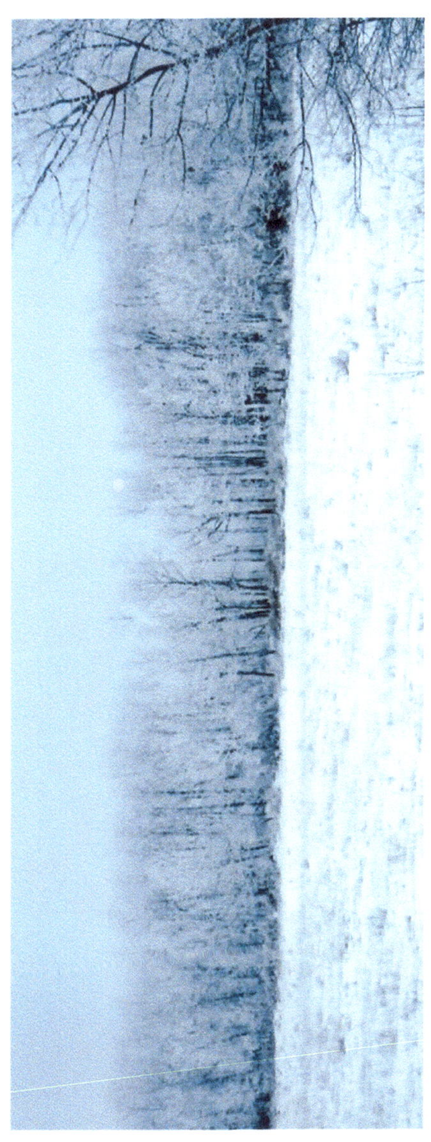

RICHARD HERRON

RICHARD HERRON

RICHARD HERRON

RICHARD HERRON

RICHARD HERRON